MW01106719

SHATTERED SAPPHIRE

A DARK ROMANCE NOVEL

D.W. MARSHALL

ISBN: 978-0-9968729-2-8

Cover design by D.W. Marshall

Edited & Interior Layout by authorsassistant.com

To all the other writers out there who get up too early and go to bed too late just get another chapter written. Don't ever stop.

PROLOGUE

I can't believe these girls. Not one of them can appreciate how good we have it here. Why would anyone want to leave this place? The Chamber is perfect. *Sex is just sex.* I mean, I have told them all this fact at least a million times. They need to seize this moment because we will not have these bodies forever. Not one of them thinks like me, but one day they will.

I have treated each day here like an answered prayer—like *I* hit the lottery. And because I'm too much of a chicken-shit to tell Mason that I want to stay, I'm being shipped home this morning with the rest of my weak sisters. Don't get me wrong, after a year of being in their presence, they have all grown on me to the point where I can really call them "sisters." Still, to say we have much in common would be a lie.

I am an island.

The only person I've ever met who I have anything in common with is Mason.

It's my own fault. There is no one else to blame but me. It's not like I have any excuses. During the past year I had nothing but time and opportunity to tell Mason that I wanted to stay, especially when he sent for me so many times during my year of welcomed captivity. In my defense, I thought we were getting serious enough that he would want to keep me. I believed that what we shared was the start of something. My pride got in the way because I obviously got it in my head that what was developing between us also meant something to him. I wanted Mason to want me to stay—I wanted him to want me. My desire was for him to show me that he felt the time we shared together was special.

Guess what? Now I'm heading home.

The other reason I think I held back is the fact that he's married to Ivory. Married. How can I mean anything to him when he already has a wife? My first night here, he commented that I could be his next wife. But what does that mean, really? *Men talk, right?* I mean, his cock was down my throat when he said it. The thing is, if I was only special enough to him to be an addition to his harem, then what we shared wasn't as important to him as I thought. *Damn.* Out of all of the men on the planet to fall in love with, I pick the most damaged—someone incapable of love.

A man like Mason lives by one code: life is about fucking.

Sure, that's my code, too, but no one can live like that forever. Even *I* expect I'll settle down at some point.

⁓

I WILL NEVER FORGET the night I was taken and brought here. My sister, Gabriella, and I were visiting relatives in Sao Paulo, Brazil. We went as often as we could in order to stay connected to our roots. Summers there were amazing. Some of the world's sexiest people gather there, and it is a nonstop party.

Gabriella and I were at what had to be the world's tiniest nightclub, right on the beach. It was so small, that if I counted, I'm sure no more than fifty people were squeezed inside, and that was including staff.

This sexy guy asked me to dance. Of course, I said yes. He was fucking fine as hell—tall, muscular, and sweaty, with the kind of humid sheen that coats your body in a cramped beach club. We dirty-danced for an hour straight. He could move, too. He did that slow grind that turns me on. When a man moves like that, you know the sex is going to be mind-blowing. I knew we were going to fuck, and I couldn't wait. When he asked me to step outside with him and take a walk on the beach, I didn't hesitate. I was going to get what I wanted.

I'm not a fan of beach sex. The idea of it is hot—the moonlight, the sand, the waves, and the beach air. But no amount of illusion is worth a week of removing sand from all the crevices of your body. I mean *all* of them. I was hoping that he had something less romantic in mind, like the back of a pickup truck. Hell, I'd even take the backseat of a car. I'm not picky.

It was on my way out with the sexy guy that everything changed. It started out innocent enough. He was holding my hand, and I was fake giggling to a joke that I only half understood because my Portuguese is rusty. All I was thinking about was him burying his cock deep inside me. I knew he was endowed, because I could feel him against me when we were dancing, and I couldn't wait. I had no idea that the seconds that followed would change a lot for me.

Some would call it the moment that life as they knew it ended, and at the time I thought the exact same thing. Suddenly, the beauty of the moonlit ocean and the multicolored lights strung along the entrance of the club no longer held the same effect of hope and promise, but were now the last images of my life. Or, so I thought.

A van pulled up in front of us, and just like a scene from a movie where the stupid girl follows a stranger out of the crowded club and into the dark night, I was shoved inside it. The only difference is, I do this shit all the time. *What can I say?* I'm sex-positive. I guess my number was finally up. I attempted to protest, but one of the three large guys inside yanked me into the van. I landed on my side and when I opened my eyes, my sister was running toward us. Another thought ran through my mind. *What if they take her, too?* I still remember my sister's horrified eyes, her mouth locked in a scream, "Em!" The sexy guy climbed into the van, slammed the door shut, and pulled out a white cloth, which he pressed up to my face. It was something straight out of a horror movie. The whole thing took minutes but felt like hours.

When I woke up, I was bound and a heavy hood covered my head. My immediate reaction was to fight. Fight for my life. Fight for my freedom. Then, the hood was removed and another emotion took over—fear.

Six other bound girls stood there. We were all scared shitless.

Then a platform rose from beneath the floor in front of us.

Mason rose up in a flood of godly light and he truly answered all of my prayers.

1

SAPPHIRE

*A*ll of my life I have never fit in. I was born into a strong Brazilian Catholic family, and I've always felt like a sinner. My sexual appetite started years before the average girl. I can't explain why. I went to church. I went through all of the steps needed to become the good little Catholic girl—my first communion, then confirmation. By confirmation, I knew that, according to the church, God didn't approve of me. But then, isn't he the one who made me the way I am?

No amount of preaching or church services helped. None of it mattered, because the feeling that goes along with being a "good" Catholic never even came close to the feeling I have when a dick is deep inside of me. Perhaps I suffer from an addiction to sex. There is such a thing. Well, if I am a nymphomaniac, I'm not ashamed. On the contrary, I'd be proud to say it to anyone.

That first night, when Mason rose from the floor and welcomed us to The Chamber, he basically told us that we would spend the next year as sex slaves. When I heard that, all the fear inside of me vanished immediately. As long as no harm came to me, I knew I would be at home in The Chamber.

My birth name is Emmanuella Maria Alves. Mason renamed me "Sapphire" that first night. Truth be told, I loved my new name. I was born to be Sapphire. Now I am bound for East Brunswick, New Jersey, and I will be stripped of my name. How can I be Emmanuella again, when being Sapphire has felt so right? Mason introduced me to a life befitting me, and I can't imagine going back.

My sisters, Gabriella and Marianna, are different. They are my mother's ideal daughters. Both of them are virgins. And me, the middle child, I'm the family slut. I wear my scarlet letter "S" with honor and shame—shame that I could never play the part of the good little Catholic girl because I love the feeling of power and euphoria that fucking gives me.

Moving from our native Brazil when I was in primary school helped, because not everyone in New Jersey is Catholic, and we were far away from our immediate family, who would only have added to the "let's judge Emmanuella" crew.

Growing up, I had friends who were also sexually mature, so hanging out with them made me feel less alone. But that was at school. Nastasia and Beth were my sidekicks, proud to be school sluts. I could share my sexual interests with others who understood me. Kids tried to label and even tease us. But we loved who we were, so we didn't give a fuck what people thought.

Home was a different story. Family is supposed to love and accept you. All of you—the good, the bad, and the ugly. I guess my parents never got that memo, because my mother always gazed upon me with disdain, and my father rarely looked at me at all.

They knew early on that I was different, and they did very little to mask how that knowledge made them feel about me. I am surprised I didn't become really screwed up. But I did have the love of my sisters, and somehow that was enough.

Don't get me wrong—I know my parents love me. They just had a really fucked up, judgmental way of showing it.

I remember my first night at The Chamber. Once we found out what was intended for us, the other girls fell apart. I guess if I was more like my sisters, I would have done the same. But I'm not. As Mason went down the line renaming us, and having us perform small sexual acts, I was excited for my turn—really excited. I wanted to jump up and down. I could not wait.

When it was finally my turn, Mason must have seen the devil in my eyes, because my act was significantly more sexual than the rest. I took his cock into my mouth with honor. I worshipped it with my tongue. I made my desire for him and this lifestyle that he was bringing me into known.

2

SAPPHIRE, THE CHAMBER

This is ridiculous. Mason has managed to summon every single girl to his chamber except me. The other girls hate it here, and if given the chance to leave, they would trample each other running for the door. They still see it as a prison, but I hope to one day call it "home." Yet, even though I've made it perfectly clear that I want to be here, I've been completely ignored.

Today is one of our days off and I'm bored. I plop down on the sofa in our common living room, annoyed.

"What's wrong, Sapphire?" Raven asks me as she sits down on the opposite end. This fierce, dark-haired Asian beauty would surely slash Mason's throat if given the opportunity.

I shrug my shoulders and shake my head in exasperation as an image of her and Mason going to town in a bed or on some sexual apparatus flashes before my eyes. "Nothing."

She leans forward, grabs the remote off of the small coffee table and flicks on the television. "Doesn't look like 'nothing' to me. But you don't have to tell me." Her attention is on the television as she says it.

I clear my throat. "How many times has Mason asked you to meet him, *privately?*"

She turns her head to regard me with skeptical eyes. "Once, and it was once too many if you ask me. I'm happy to report that I'm not one of his favored. You?"

I sigh with the thought that I, too, might not be favored. "He hasn't asked for me at all."

Her eyebrow hitches up. "Really? But you're so..." she lets the words fall.

"So, what?" I fix my face with a lip twist and an eyebrow furrow.

She shrugs. "Eager to be here."

"That's...true. I love it here. It feels more like home than mine ever did. I'm surprised *you* haven't plotted an elaborate escape. You're always watching and analyzing. I see you, girl."

She cracks a rare smile.

"Don't know where I'd go if I did. This place is an island. Water surrounds us on most sides."

I hitch my eyebrow up at her. "How can you possibly know that?"

She scoffs. "I'm an islander. I can smell the sea in the air, even through all this stone. I can feel it in my body, and when its quiet, I can hear the waves." She turns her attention back to the television. "Besides running would be a fool's mission. This guy is organized. Best to wait it out. I have little sisters at home to keep safe."

"The accommodations ain't too shabby either. You feel me?" I say.

She nods slowly. "It could be worse."

"Sorry to interrupt, ladies."

We turn to find my groomer, Levi behind us.

"Hey, Levi," Raven and I say at the same time. Levi is sweet. He has a handsome face, with soft brown eyes and dark blond hair. He is good at his job—keeping me primped and chamber-ready. He steps closer to us, but remains quiet. What does he want? Because it's always something.

"I'll leave you," Raven says in a rush as she hops up and walks away.

Levi takes her spot on the sofa and stares at me with a quizzical smile on his face.

"What?" I ask. I can feel my eyes squint in confusion.

He remains silent.

I roll my eyes at him. "I don't play guessing games. If you have words, kindly slide them onto the tip of your tongue and spit them out."

"His grace would like to see you now."

Inwardly my stomach turns with excitement. My heart kicks up a beat, thrumming inside my chest. Outwardly, I turn away from him and say, "Tell *your* grace I have plans."

He scoffs, causing me to turn to him. "What?" I ask and stare at him under furrowed brows. "I'm serious. I've been here for six months without a word from him and he wants to see me now? Well, he can just wait."

"It's funny, you say that like you actually have a choice," he says.

I shrug. "I do."

He tilts his head to study me. "So, you're telling me that you're not Mason's captive until he decides otherwise?"

"Yup."

He purses his lips in disbelief. "Let me get this straight, you believe that you can walk out any time you wish?"

I deadpan. "That is not what I said or meant."

He rolls his eyes and lets out a heavy breath.

I continue. "It's a matter of distinction. The other girls don't want to be here. You know they would bolt if they could. But I wouldn't, if given the chance I would beg to stay. I'm hardly a captive. But, if he wants to ignore me for months and then summon me out of the blue then he can come and get me his damn self."

He stares at me with admiration in his eyes. "*Or*, I could drag you there."

I nod slowly. "You could. But you won't." I smile.

His face changes and the sweetness returns. "No, I won't." He smiles at me and plants a kiss on my cheek. "You, my dear, are a pain in my ass."

He rises from the couch.

"Where are you headed?" I ask hiding the smile of victory between tight lips.

"To tell Mason of your treachery."

He makes a face at me and mumbles on his way out of the room, something about dull moments never happening around me.

The second he is out of sight I allow the smile on my face to take over. Mason is finally calling for me. I know there has to be a reason, but if I am going to remain here after the other girls leave, I have to make him want me to stay.

3

SAPPHIRE, THE CHAMBER

*I*t takes thirty minutes before Mason is standing in the family room of our Chambermaid suite, with his dark eyes and chiseled features, sucking all of the oxygen out of the room. He's always in a suit, but in my imagination, I rip it off to unlock the secret treasures hidden underneath. "Bristling" is the best way I can describe his energy as it bounces around the room. His lips are in a tight line, but his eyes dance with amusement.

Who is she? They probe.

We are alone in the room. Less than ten feet separate us. We both assess and study each other. I refuse to fidget and give up any of the ground that brought him to me. I match him stare for stare.

He lets out a heavy breath and I see his body relax. "What do have to say for yourself?" His eyes are intense as he waits for my reply.

I dip my head down and inhale. I fix my face in what I hope is a neutral expression before locking eyes with him. "It's about fucking time," I say on an exhale.

The smile that grows on his face is slow and delicious. He

understands something about me now. He must know it's not just a rumor that I want to be here. He extends his hand and I cross the room to hold it. I've never been a blusher, or maybe I have been all this time, but no man has ever caused that reaction in me. When Mason smiles down at me and gives my hand a soft squeeze, my cheeks warm, then blaze.

As we cross through The Chamber, we pass people along the way, they react to the sight of Mason and I walking down the halls as if this is a normal everyday occurrence. By the looks of surprise and confusion on their faces I imagine this is a Chamber first.

After weaving through long corridors and dark stair-cases, we come to a stop in front of an enormous door. My breath catches in my throat in anticipation. In a move straight out of a spy movie, he places his hand on a biometric pad for scanning. The door makes a whisking sound as it slides open. Mason pulls at my hand to guide me inside, but I don't move. He turns to look at me with question in his eyes.

"Have you brought the other girls here?" I ask, not breaking eye contact. He already sees me differently. Unless he makes a habit of holding hands with his chambermaids all the time. *I am different.*

He smiles at me. "You are the first. I have two Chambers, but this one is special."

My wide face-splitting smile is my gift to him.

His boyish laugh that follows is mine.

I follow him inside without another second of hesitation. The space is as lavish as the rest of The Chamber, but kicked up a notch. Old world stone walls and floors meet shiny black, sleek leather furniture. Glass chandeliers hang from the ceiling throwing sparkling light around the room. His bed is fit for "his grace"—massive with a high black leather head-board and white and gray bedding.

There is so much distance between us. He's deep within the room and I'm hovering on its perimeter, taking it all in.

Being here alone with him speaks volumes, and if I do all the right things, maybe he'll keep me.

Wanting something is a feeling I am unaccustomed to. The uncertainty feels like sour milk sitting in the bottom of my stomach. But I want this—the man, the place, the life. In truth, I barely know Mason Wilde, but something about him speaks to me on a visceral plane. When he rose from the floor on my first day here, I just knew I wanted him to be mine.

"Nice place," I say as if I see rooms as beautiful as this all the time.

He lets out a breathy laugh, but he stays rooted in place; I do the same. I continue glancing at him, then the room. My heart is running its own race, beating so hard and fast I can hear it pounding in my ears. My stomach is in uncomfortable knots.

Gone is the ultra-confident man who'd gone down our line of seven and named us. *Is this the real Mason?* He's guarded and cautious, his chest rises and falls fast as he regards me.

I turn my attention away from him and toward the glass wall at the back of his room. Raven is right about the water. The castle backs up to a sharp cliff edge, greener than anything I've ever seen, and then to deep water as far as the eyes can see.

It's a beautiful dream.

I take cautious steps into the room, Mason doesn't move. When I get to him I let out a breath, stopping to stare into his eyes, but I continue past him, positioning myself as close to the glass as I can physically get without actually touching it. It takes my breath away.

The sound of a door opening catches my attention. When I turn to the sound, I see that he has opened an exterior door. He wordlessly walks through, leaving it open for me to follow. I couldn't hold in the gasp if I wanted to. It has been six months since I have been outside. The only breezes I've felt have come from skylights or the tiniest of windows. He is giving me something precious—his trust.

The air is sweeter than anything I have ever experienced, made sweeter by the mix of fragrant blossoms and the sea. The grass is thick and lush as I walk through it to stand at his side. When I turn to inspect The Chamber, I see that it is every bit of the castle that the interior suggests it to be, with vines and colorful flowers crawling up the sides. The breeze tickles my skin and I suddenly have the desire for it to touch every inch of me.

Mason is closer to me now, an arm's reach away. I move my hands to my shoulders and slide my dress strap from one shoulder, then the next. My eyes are trained on his as my sapphire sheath dress falls into a puddle on the grass at my feet. He never signals for me to stop, and I'm not sure that I'd listen. Instead he watches my every movement, his eyes giving nothing away. Maybe I see a hint of something.... Longing? I step out of my dress and close my eyes as the air dances across my skin. My nipples tighten from the contact and a moan escapes me. When I open my eyes, Mason is staring down at me in awe.

He closes the distance, his fingers are unsure as they make contact, touching my cheek, running a trail down my throat. He draws slow circles on my shoulder, his eyes never leaving mine. My breath catches in my throat. *Who is this shy man?* From what I've heard from the other girls, he was rough and aggressive, not smooth and tender.

"Where did you come from?" His voice is soft.

"New Jersey."

His lips crash into mine. It is dizzying how he takes his time, tasting my lips, sucking and pulling them into his mouth, before parting my lips and sinking his tongue inside. Our tongues dance together to music that isn't there. His hands never wander, no matter how badly I want them to. He pulls me closer, and my bare body presses against his clothing. Hidden muscles reveal themselves as they collide against me. My thighs ache from squeezing them so tight to suppress the yearning between my legs. I break the kiss to take a breath and I am delighted when his lips find mine again. Who knew a sweet kiss could feel like this? I have never done "sweet" before. I have had sex with all of the thirty-five lottery winners since my arrival months ago, and I have not felt satisfied. But somehow this kiss is more satisfying than anything I have experienced to date. *How can that be?*

Before I get lost in his kisses, he breaks contact. He locks eyes with me, his expression cautious and frustrated. His breathing is fast and hard, matching mine. He is forcing himself to resist me. I can see it there on his face—lust and desire at war with restraint and trepidation. Why?

He leans down and snatches my dress up from the grass, then lets out a long breath. When he reaches for my hand I give it to him freely, and we walk back into his room. I am hopeful that we are heading straight to his massive bed. Once inside his demeanor changes, and caution gives way to irritation. *Mercurial Mason.* Since arriving at his chamber, he has been sweet, nervous, almost shy, and lustful. Now he's angry? *Way to keep me off balance.*

He hands me my dress. "Please get dressed, Emmanuella," he says, but doesn't look at me.

"I thought I was Sapphire—" His glare cuts me off, causing my heart to crawl into my throat. What's left of my usual confidence and swagger oozes through my pores, chilling my body. This is so weird. He has had sex with all of the other chambermaids, some more than a few times, and after a simple kiss and barely a touch, he won't even look at me. What's so wrong with me that the man who created a sex chamber would want nothing to do with me?

Tears balance on the rim of my eyes as I work my dress back on. *Do not cry, Em, not in front of him.* I focus on my breathing, and take slow measured breaths. I can't show this man how important this moment is to me. My hands shake while I'm dressing. He gives me the impression that he favors strength over weakness, but after today, who knows? He has me so confused. Once dressed, I cross my arms in front of my body, hugging myself and attempting to calm my emotions. The energy between us is another entity in the room— colliding with me, causing my heart to race, breaths to turn shallow, and the tiny hairs on my skin to stand tall.

Our glances go from outright stares to avoiding each other altogether. A chime echoes through the room and Mason jumps to attention, as if he was in a daze. I watch him walk hastily across the room. He opens the door and greets our visitor, a man dressed in white serving attire.

"Pierre, thank you for putting this together on such short notice."

The man nods to me and his smile is warm and sincere. "Anytime, Mason, sir."

I stand rooted in my spot and watch with curiosity as Pierre pulls lid after lid from small serving trays of meats and cheese, fruits and vegetables, and breads. The fragrances lift into the air and my stomach growls with want. Once he has placed the food within reach of an intimate table for two, he reaches under the cart and pulls out a bucket with a wine bottle sticking out, followed by another. He uncorks them and places them on the table with the food.

I watch the spectacle before me, wondering what Mason's game is. I steal a couple of glances at Mason and he is watching me. His expression is unreadable.

"Thank you, Pierre," Mason says once the table is set, but his eyes are on mine.

"Will there be anything else?" Pierre asks.

"That will be all, Pierre," Mason's eyes drop from my face and trail down to my bare feet, then back up. "Everything looks perfect." His lips curve almost imperceptibly upward.

Pierre makes clanging noises as he gathers up his things. I haven't broken eye contact with Mason, trying to read him at every turn. What is he up to?

My mind is saying, *please want me* over and over on a loop.

It's a strange intrusive thought. I've never cared if a man wanted me for anything more than sex, because for me, that was all they were good for, too. I try to block the thought, hoping my expression isn't dopey and hopeful. I can't give him anything when he isn't giving me as much as a hint that he wants to do anything with me except eat a meal.

Pierre says a final goodbye, and the atmosphere in the room changes the second he shuts the door. My breaths are more shallow than before, and my head swims. I reach for the closest of the chairs because I need to sit down.

"Please, allow me." Mason rushes to pull out the seat for me. I will my legs to deposit me into the seat, determined to see this through. Mason pushes my seat in closer to the table, before taking a seat across from me. *How am I so bad at this? How is he?*

I watch as he pulls this and that from the serving trays and piles everything onto our plates. I pluck a red grape from the vine and pop it into my mouth, licking the sweet juice from my lips. Mason's eyes fall to my mouth and his forms a hard line. *WTF?* I'd expected by now we'd be on our third course of fucking in every position—on the floor, on the bed, attached to some medieval apparatus, his cock buried so deep inside of me that I would taste him on my tongue. But, instead, we're on a *date?*

"How has your stay been, Emmanuella?"

Again with the Emmanuella shit?

I look up at him, doing my best to keep my expression neutral. A sharp response is on the tip of my tongue, but I select another. "Delightful." I pair a square of cheese with a salami disc and take a bite.

"I must tell you, the lottery winners can't say enough about how much they enjoy their time with you." He takes a long draw of sparkling white wine, peering down the glass at me.

My intention is to smile with my eyes, not in flirtation, but with genuine happiness to be here. I'm not sure which emotion I convey. "Well, it is my aim to please." I turn my attention to my plate. Between the pleasant conversation, formal table, and so much eye contact, this ruse is wearing me out. *Sheesh.* I'm betting he is studying me every bit as much as I am him.

All this "normal" has me off-kilter. Heck, I've already gotten naked in front of him, and now I have my clothes back on. This is so not how I saw the night going.

Mason sighs and causes me to look up at him.

"Yes. Some of the men have asked for extra time with you."

"Really?" I say, though I'm not surprised.

One of his eyebrows hitches up and his eyes are laser-focused on mine. "I denied their requests, of course."

Interesting. I narrow my eyes at him.

"Was I incorrect? Should I have said yes? You'd be quite busy if I did." His expression gives nothing away.

I shrug and return his focused attention. "I mean, what else would I do with my extra time around here?"

Mason looks down at his plate. "I see. Well, I guess I could tell them you're available after all." When he looks up, he has a crestfallen expression. It's the first time he's given me some sort of indication he cares. He wants me to say no, he may even need me to.

I sit up straighter in my seat. "I didn't say that I *wanted* to participate in any extracurricular activities with any lottery winners."

His eyes grow smaller as he gazes into mine. "You don't?"

I shake my head. "Look, Mason. I appreciate how you've gone out of your way for me today. The private chambers, the fresh air, the hand-holding, and this spread. But can I ask you a question?"

His lips curl into a small smile. I do the same.

"Of course."

I let out a breath. "What am I doing here? I mean, like this? You ignore me for six months and when you do finally call upon me, you don't even want me. Is there something wrong with me?"

He laughs.

I've asked him the most pressing question, something I have wondered for months as he's favored the other girls over me. Why am I not enough? And he laughs. If I wasn't so determined to get my answer, I think I would slap his face.

"That's just it, I do want you." His eyes brighten. "I'm not good at flowery romance shit. I've never had to be, and I certainly never wanted to be." He exhales on a sigh and stares at me for a long time, it seems like his words are hanging on the tip of his tongue. "You scare the shit out of me."

I squeeze my eyes shut and digest what he just said. "Me? This whole time I thought you were pissed at me and I had no idea what I could have done."

He rests his arms on the table. "I want more with you than I ever wanted before. That's what scares me. But I can't keep avoiding this…you. I'm not capable of a relationship, you have to know that. But I'd very much like to spend time with you while you are here. I thought if I stayed away from you the feelings would go away. I fought the need and want and it only got worse." His eyes narrow and crinkle in the corners, suggesting that this is the hardest thing he has ever said before.

"Wait. I'm confused. So, you're saying you want to date me?"

He reaches across the table and takes my hand. My body tingles with excitement that is foreign to me. I don't say anything, hoping that he will continue.

"I decided today would be the day. To just see. Maybe I was imagining more than what was there. But the second we were alone I knew I wanted more. This is strange for me."

"Ha," I laugh. "Me, too."

My blush matches his. Here we are, two sex addicts, skating into unfamiliar territory.

"What do you say, Emmanuella? You up for spending your free time getting to know me?"

"I think I can squeeze you in, if you stop calling me Emmanuella." I say and smile at him.

He nods. "How about this? We can be August and Emmanuella when we are alone and Mason and Sapphire around everyone else."

"That name suits you."

We spend the rest of our afternoon exchanging polite conversation. My eyes wander over to the bed and he catches me a couple of times and laughs. I will not get to be sexed up by Mason today, and I have no idea when I will get to explore a day or night with him between my legs. This sex addict, it seems, wants to take it slow with me.

But he trusted me with his real name. That has to mean something big.

4

MASON, THE CHAMBER

I can only imagine the questions that are headed my way after being seen walking Emmanuella to and from my private chamber holding her hand. I even escorted her back to her section of The Chamber.

Now I need to seek out counsel. I feel crazy inside with emotions. Hope? I haven't experienced that shit since I was a kid. My parents taught me young with their constant failed promises—hope leads to shit and disappointment. By ten, my motto was "fuck hope, wishing, or dreaming." I pull out the two-way and dial Tyson's line.

"Yeah, boss?" his voice breaks through the static.

"You got a minute to have a drink in the study?" I ask and wait for his response.

"Sure. See you there in five."

"Copy. Five, then."

I take a left at the end of the hall toward the study, surely he can talk some sense into me. He's falling for Flame, and I'm sure if he could prevent those feelings, he would. For guys like me and Tyson, relationships are a hinderance. The more people you love, the more you risk losing. I don't have anyone in my life that I'd risk everything for. Loved ones are the main reason the women I take don't try to escape. I don't threaten the women. Showing them that I can get to the people they love any time I want—video after video of them at home, with their families, at work or school—buys absolute compliance. The more people you love, the more you have to lose and the more you'll sacrifice to prevent it.

"Hey. Everything okay, boss?" Tyson asks walking into the study. "You look...stressed."

"Ha. I'll say. Have a drink with me." I walk behind the bar, pull a beer out of the fridge for him, and pour myself a neat whiskey. We take a seat on the bar stools.

"I met with her today," I say.

"Her who?" He asks and takes a long draw from his bottle.

Before I let him in on what happened today, I take a gulp and the amber liquid heats my throat and stomach. "Sapphire. I brought her to my *private* chamber. We...had a *sexless* date."

He looks at me like I've gone crazy. "Wow, okay. I'd heard a few murmurs in the halls that you were holding hands with a chambermaid, but I didn't believe it. How'd it feel?"

"Man, it's too much. I think I made a mistake." I scoff. "I can't be doing this shit. Look around you, I'm not the guy that gets the girl and the sappy ending."

"I've done terrible things, too."

Is he fucking kidding me? His mother was gunned down in front of him when he was a kid and the worst thing he ever did was work for the government. I give him a measured look. "Killing for your country—"

"It's still killing. It still fucks you up in here." He points to his head then turns away from me, picking up his beer and taking a draw. The silence sits in the air between us like a thick fog. Tyson takes a deep breath, exhales, and the fog seems to clear. "And let's not forget, I'm here working with you. I may not have created this place, but I'm a big part of it." He shrugs. "Who says you don't get to have someone to share your life with? Hell, some of the worst criminal minds in history had wives and families."

Panic rushes through me.

"How? I've gone my whole life not worrying about anything or anyone and I'm already in trouble with her. I want to pull her from the lineup." I stare into his eyes, I see them narrow as he stares at me. He'd once begged me not to bring Flame here a full year before it would be her time, and I'd denied him. If I yanked Sapphire from her duties, he would never forgive me, and I respect him.

"I'm not a hypocrite, I would never do that to you. She stays in the lineup, but it's a throat punch every time. Now I know how you feel. I'm sorry I did that shit to you."

"Thanks. Yeah, you are some sort of a genius with the two-year surveillance, but it seems that shit backfired on us." He holds up his bottle to clink it with mine, and we both laugh.

"Maybe if I ever loved someone I could have understood where you were coming from."

He leans back and looks at me. "Come on, man. You gotta love somebody. Parents?"

"Sure, I have them, but 'tolerate' is a better way to describe our relationship. No love there."

"Siblings?"

I sigh. "Only fucking child."

"Damn, Mason. So whatcha gonna do?"

"Fuck if I know. What do you do?"

His jaws clench and his eyes show their pain. "I watch her with every man that walks into her chamber."

"How? And more importantly, why?"

He harrumphs. "If I love her, I have to suffer with her. It's the only way I can stay here with her. My heart breaks every single time, but I do it anyway." He looks away. "Sapphire's different, though. She seems to be enjoying herself. It shouldn't be too hard to watch." Realization floods his face. "I take that back."

I let out a heavy breath. "I never said I loved her. I…I think I want to see what *more* feels like."

He laughs. "Have you two had sex?"

I shake my head.

He laughs harder and pats my shoulder. "Damn, Mason, you've got it worse than I thought."

I hop off the stool and go behind the bar to refill my glass and grab him another beer. "What should I do?" I ask handing him his bottle.

He shrugs. "She's here for six more months. I say let it play out. I'd also watch her feeds if I was you. If seeing her with another man makes you want to go break his head open then it might just be love."

"You know you suck, right?"

"I know. I'll have that feed in your room tonight," he says and downs his beer.

5

MASON, THE CHAMBER

*T*onight is Sapphire's first night inside her chamber since our date. Tyson not only set up a feed into my room, he made sure the monitor was so fucking big, I could see every detail from across the room. "Thanks a lot, asshole!" I yell into the dark void and turn my attention to her. Her chamber is empty at the moment. I just see her electric blue sheets on her canopy bed and her furnishings. I wait impatiently for her to appear on screen. And when she does, my stomach drops. *She is extraordinary.*

Levi styled her in lingerie—a sheer blue camisole, matching lacy thong, and stockings that come to a stop at her thighs and are clipped into place, making her naturally tanned skin appear deeper. Her dark hair falls over her shoulders in big dramatic waves. Her back is to me and her ass is firm and round. My dick stirs in my pants, growing with want. This is going to be bad.

The first man enters her chamber. It's Radley. I hate him already for what is about to happen. He's in his late forties, tall and thin with dark blond hair. Radley is the foreign leader of a billion-dollar corporation in Europe. This is actually his third time participating in a chamber. He is one of the many who live here the entire year, slipping away for a week here or there for business obligations.

When he strips out of his clothes, his dick is already hard and ready. I clench my fists. The only thought in my brain is *don't touch her.* She walks toward him, her ass swinging in approach. When she is standing in front of him, she drops to her knees and takes his dick into her mouth. His head falls back and he reaches out for one of her bedposts. Loud moans escape him and I want to rip his throat out.

Sapphire pushes him onto the bed. He watches her as she undresses. "You want this hot pussy?" she asks.

Radley nods his head fast.

"What are you going to do with it?" Her voice is silk and air. My dick is so hard it aches, but I refuse to give it what it wants. *What the hell is wrong with me?*

"I'm going fuck the bloody hell out of it."

She shakes her head. "Not until you've eaten. You look like a very hungry boy and my pussy needs some attention. Now lie down."

He follows her instructions and she walks around the bed, climbs on, and sinks her pussy onto his face. "Eat, Daddy."

I watch in horror as my girl grinds her pussy onto him, rubbing her tits, and moaning. When she leans forward and takes his dick into her mouth, I can't take it anymore, and I flick the monitor off.

"This is some bullshit." My dick is so hard that each step hurts as I leave my room and head for the chambers. What I'll do when I get there...I have no fucking idea. But I can't just sit there and watch her. I must look a sight, storming through the halls with my dick threatening to spit my pants open. People clear a path for me, and I don't speak. My heart is racing, my skin is hot and flushed.

When I arrive in the great circular room, the entrance to her chamber is open, they all are. Dark stairs lead up to bright and colorful sex rooms I created.

"Boss?" Weaver asks in obvious confusion. He is the guard at the base of her chamber. When I glance around the room, the other six guards are watching me. In seven years, I have never entered a room to check on them. Sure, when we first set The Chamber up I'd keep an eye on things to make sure we were running smoothly. Tyson does the security checks around here. So my presence is probably confusing. When I look up at the computer screen, Sapphire and Radley are going at it, he's on top and he is pounding the shit out of her. I clench my jaw and watch. She pushes him off of her, turns over onto her hands and knees arching her back, and he plunges into her.

"Boss, what are you down here?" Camp asks. Like the other guards, he is strong, fit, and military-trained.

"Just checking things out. Why is the sound down?" I take measured breaths in an attempt to slow my racing heart down. Now, to make sure I don't look like an ass, I have to check in on everybody else.

Before I can step away, Sapphire's guard nudges me.

"Sapphire is a fucking beast. I usually come five or six times watching her fuck," Camp says. I resist the sudden urge to kick his ass and break a
few bones.

"You are not here to get off. You are assigned to protect her."

"But, boss. That means the only time I get to enjoy my post is when she falls asleep, and she never does."

I hold out my hand to shut him up then make my way around the room.

"How's Violet tonight, Gabe?"

"She's doing great, boss." I look at the camera and she is on her pleasure pony. The pony is on its lowest setting. Her feet are on the pegs and she is grinding the dildo while she sucks the lottery winner's dick.

"So, we can't jack off while we watch anymore?" Gabe asks. "If that's the case, you are gonna have some grouchy-ass guards, boss. I'm gonna need something to fuck." He looks up at me and his expression says it all. He's right, I can't ask them to do this and not relieve themselves. The truth is, I don't care what the others do, I really only meant that for Camp, but even that would come off wrong. I walk over to Tyson.

"How's Flame tonight?" Out of respect for him I don't watch her feed. *Who the hell am I?* That is shit I am not accustomed to caring about.

"She's all right. I'm keeping an eye on her. You okay, man? You never come down here."

I turn my back to the monitor and stare down at him in his chair to make a point of letting him know I am not watching his girl fuck another man. He gives me a tight nod of appreciation. I lean close and say in a low voice intended only for him, "Man, I tried to watch the feed in my room and I nearly blew a gasket. I tore out of my room, and this is where I ended up. I think I'm losing my shit."

He pats my arm firmly, but it's comforting. "You'll manage. You've just got to figure out how to exist in this crazy-ass space while falling in love."

I stare daggers at him. "I'm not—" But I don't finish the thought because I can't really say what I am. "You know you suck, right?"

"Yeah, yeah, but you know I'm right."

I flip him off and he laughs. "Hey, how's Serge been behaving?"

"Like a boy scout."

"Good to hear. Glad our little 'talk' helped him see reason. Talk to you later?"

"Sure."

My next chamber is Sky's. "Tolliver, how's Sky tonight?"

He gives me a big smile. "See for yourself."

I turn my attention to her feed. She is suspended from a swing, moving slowly forward and back, her pink pussy glistening in the camera. My dick contracts and thickens in my pants.

"Where's the lottery winner?"

"Oh he's coming. This guy likes to watch, has a cream pie fetish."

He comes into view, dick in hand. He rubs and strokes it hard and fast. When his milk spills, he pushes his dick inside of her, and immediately pulls it back out. He takes his fingers and separates her lips to watch his come spill out of her. He pushes back inside of her and pounds her like a cracked-out rabbit.

"That was...different," I say and watch in fascination as his body clenches and shakes, pressing hard and deep inside of her. When he pulls out he spreads her open and waits until his white cream oozes out again. *This guy really likes his stuff.* I shake my head and walk to Raven's guard, Jacob.

"How's Raven tonight?"

He scoffs. "Scary, as usual. She fucks with military precision. Definitely not enjoying herself."

When I look at the feed, I can see that he is right. She stares into the camera like she just might cut the person on the other side. In six months, she hasn't acclimated to this life. She is a robot. She has removed herself emotionally from the job. Still, I have received no complaints.

"Well, keep an eye on her. In this case, I'm more worried about the men than her."

Jacob laughs. "I'll bet."

Usually, I think of myself as a genius, and move through the halls of The Chamber with pride and an energy that says I am on top of the world. Not today. Not this time. My stomach is tight, my energy is all wrong. Something feels...*off.*

I move to the next guard, Money. "What's going on with Sunshine tonight?"

"She is right as rain, boss."

She is with Connell tonight. If I didn't know better, I'd say they were lovers under the covers, with a lot more kissing than usual. "Those two are getting cozy, eh?"

"I'll say."

With not much to see on her feed, I move down to Ivy. She is proving to be much more fragile than I would have expected. I speak to her guard, Tolliver, and move quickly to the center of the room.

"Listen, sorry for the intrusion. You all are doing an amazing job of keeping the women safe. I misspoke earlier, feel free to whip out your dicks and have a good time." The men laugh as I make my way back to Camp.

"Thanks, boss," he says.

"Yeah, no problem. But—" I lean in close to him. "If she falls asleep in her chamber and you so much as touch a hair on her head, I will break your back."

He stares up at me with fear in his eyes and swallows hard and loud. "Understood."

I pat him on the back and make my way out of the room.

6

SAPPHIRE, THE CHAMBER

*I*t's not long before Mason invites me back to his private chamber. This time he doesn't come and get me, but sends a female by the name of Reza. She's tall and pretty, like an indie rock artist, with bright tattoos covering her fair skin and long white hair.

He answers the door wearing a smoking jacket with bare legs, suggesting that he might be naked underneath. *Oh, I hope so.* "Come in," he swings his arm to let us pass.

"Thank you, Reza," I say.

I make my way deeper into his room, but Reza stays near the door.

"That will be all, Reza," Mason says.

I don't turn to watch her exit, but I hear the door close behind her.

"She's nice," I say and walk closer to him.

"I'm glad you like her." He makes his way to me, until we are close enough to touch, a small step is all that's left between us. He inhales and closes his eyes. His chest rises and falls, slow and hard. "You smell divine."

"Thank you."

He reaches out for my hand and I give it to him. He turns in silence and I follow him to the back of his room and out the door.

The sea air is cooler today against my bare arms and gooseflesh dots my skin. Mason takes off his robe and wraps it around me. I am disappointed to see him in an undershirt and boxer briefs.

"Thank you."

We stare out at the sea. The waves are rolling, birds skim the surface. It calms my soul.

I turn to him. "Why did Reza come to get me instead of Levi?"

He doesn't answer me and I don't push. This is a strange situation for both of us. The question is out there and I hope he will answer it soon.

"It's chilly, let's get you back inside."

I follow him back into the room and to his massive sofa.

"What is it like for you being with the lottery winners?" he asks.

I shrug, tucking my legs underneath me and turning so that I'm facing him. "What do you mean? Are you asking me if I like it?"

He nods.

"I mean, I like sex." I take a moment. "Or are you asking me if I would trade thirty-five men for one sex-crazed man?"

He pauses and stares into my eyes. He is maddening. His hand rubs my leg absently. "The latter." The words are slow and deliberate.

"In a heartbeat. Back home I wasn't into stuff like this. I mean, I'm game and this has been a great experience, but I'd take the sex-crazed guy. Like this." I snap my fingers.

The smile on his face makes my stomach do somersaults.

"I watched you the other night."

My eyes grow wide. "And?"

Pained eyes meet mine. "It nearly killed me." His fingers play with mine and his eyes drop to our entwined hands. My heartbeat kicks up with the notion of him struggling to watch me and the idea that something is happening between us. We're sex addicts slowing things down for the possibility of…*what?*

I stare at our hands, too, my breath shaky as it leaves my body.

"I grew angrier by the second, and before I knew it, I was racing down to…to… I don't even know what." He squeezes his eyes shut then opens them.

"When I got to the base of your chamber, I was on the verge of losing it. I told your guard that if you fall asleep and he lays one hand on you I will break his neck." He blows out a heavy breath and sighs. Our eyes connect, then his dart from mine, to our hands, back to me, and around the room.

"I want to take you off the line. I want to fold this place up, simply because I can't stand the idea of someone else touching you." His eyes stop on mine and his expression hardens. "I want to send you home and forget I ever met you, because you are ruining everything for me."

Panic runs through me at those words. I don't want to go home. I belong here with him. But to say this out loud might freak him out enough to send me packing.

"So what are you going to do about everything that's running through your mind?"

He opens his arms and pulls me against him. "Nothing today. I don't think I'm strong enough to let you go, at least right now. So, I'd like to continue to get to know you, Emmanuella. You are a beguiling creature and I can't seem to get enough."

I smile undetected in his arms.

"I replaced Levi with Reza, because I am a controlling lunatic that doesn't like the idea of any man touching you. I may not be able to control what happens inside your chamber, but I can damn sure control who grooms you."

That admission warrants another smile.

"So, how long are we going to treat this like the prehistoric times where you court me?"

He throws his head back and laughs.

"Oh, trust me, if this were the caveman days, I'd have drug you in here by your hair months ago and buried my dick so deep inside of you, you wouldn't be able to walk for days. You're thinking of the fifties."

I pull away from him and stare into his eyes. "I like the sound of the caveman days."

Without asking permission, I straddle him. He gasps in surprise and I bring his open mouth to mine. I take my time, savoring the simplicity of our lips entwined, breath on skin, wetness, and the tip of his tongue on mine. Our moans tell tales of what we want. His cock grows beneath me as my hips dance, pushing mine to his. I run my fingers through his dark hair, pulling him so close that I can't tell which pounding heart is my own. I am falling for this man, for his restraint and pushback, his desire, and his control. My mouth, my fingers, and my body beg him to want me forever.

7

MASON, THE CHAMBER

A month has gone by and I am nowhere closer to figuring this shit out. I watch Sapphire by night inside of her chamber,

fucking men and calling them "Daddy." I have lost hair in frustration.

During the day, she is Emmanuella and I am August. We shy away from talk of her activities inside her chamber. Instead, we talk and kiss and lay in the tall grass and listen to the waves crash against the rocks. We are finding some normal in this craziness. Who knew I would ever want or appreciate this?

Tonight, I take my usual front row seat to watch her *work*.

When Serge walks in, my chest tightens. He has been behaving himself, according to Tyson, but every time I see him with her it sets me on edge. He is a creepy, rich bastard. Most of the men here can have sex with anyone they want, but they pay for the anonymity, the exotic experience, the game. Unfortunately, I think Serge is here because no amount of money would cause women to flock to him.

He stands before her naked, his chest puffed out and his

dick ready. She doesn't look as happy as she does with the others. The good news is, he doesn't stay in the chambers long. She starts by taking his dick into her hands, stroking him.

"Put Serge's cock into your mouth and suck it hard." *He's referring to himself in the third person?*

She does as he asks.

"Harder, girl!" he shouts. His hand grabs her by the head.

She looks up at him, wincing. That asshole is hurting her. He is not going to harm anyone of my chambermaids again. I take off for the round room. The bruises he left on Flame were his first strike and that's the only one he gets. I should have kicked his ass out.

I depress the two-way. "Tyson, I'm heading down there. I think Serge might be going there again. Check the feed."

"On it, boss."

I'm not in an all-out run, because I know that Tyson or any one of the guards will be up those stairs and beating his ass if he gets too rough, but I am moving fast.

"Looks okay to me, boss."

My breaths are coming out hard and fast when I make my way to the round room. I don't even check the feed, instead I take the stairs three at a time. I hear her call him Daddy and my stomach turns. When I cross the threshold, she is on her knees and he is bucking and shaking behind her. Both of them are shocked by my appearance. Sapphire scrambles away from him and covers herself with blankets.

I am so out of breath I can't speak. Half from running and the other from working myself into a frenzy.

"Everything okay here?" I ask.

"Dah, everything is fine. I fucked her good and now I go to sleep."

"I must be in the wrong chamber, my apologies," I lie.

Serge pulls his clothes back on, walks up to me, and extends his hand for me to shake. When I don't take his extended hand, he laughs it off and slaps my shoulder. "You throw good party here, Mason. You Americans, so worried all the time. Relax, you'll live longer. See you soon, sweet Sapphire." The words trail behind him, leaving the two of us staring at each other.

I depress the two-way for Camp. "Cut the feed."

"Yes, boss. Feed is cut."

"Are you okay?" I ask, slitting my eyes.

She nods.

"Miss Sapphire, your bath is—" Reza pauses when she sees me.

I hold up my hand to her. "Everything is fine, Reza. Sometimes Serge can get a little rough and I needed to make sure." I extend my hand out to Sapphire and she is slow but climbs off the bed and takes it. She keeps herself covered in a sheet, not saying anything. The second her hand is in mine, my heart and breathing slow down. I am losing my shit for sure. But to look at her and see her now, after spending so much time together, she is so much more than her exotic beauty.

I expect her to follow me to her bath, instead she folds into my arms and I wrap my arms around her and kiss the top of her head. "I'm okay," she says.

She lets me go and walks away, stopping in the doorway to the bathroom. "Do yourself and me a favor and stop watching my feeds, it's making you crazy." She winks at me and disappears.

I stare after her for a spell, not sure if she will appear in the doorway again. When I am satisfied that she won't, I turn to head down the stairs.

"Hey."

When I turn around Reza is standing in the chamber. "She's a tough girl."

I shrug. "I know." Worrying about her is a tug-of-war that is breaking me down.

"As for that asshole, we have a code word. Purple. If she yells purple, I come running out and clock him in the head with this." She holds up a bat encased in foam. "Not hard enough to kill him, but he'll wake up with a mother of a headache."

I nod my approval. "I knew I chose well with you. Thank you." I walk out of her chamber.

~

TWO HOURS LATER, there is a knock on my door. I'm not expecting anyone, but I hurry to open it.

"Have you gone crazy?" Tyson shouts at me. "You have lost all perspective." He rushes into my private suite, unplugs the monitor, and wraps the cords around it. I watch in silence as he walks everything to the door and sets it down, but doesn't leave. He turns to me.

"I know. I know. I fucked up," I say before he can.

He lets out a breath. "No more feed. No more round room." He stands and stares at me. As my head of security, his opinion is the most valuable to me.

Tyson visibly relaxes and flops onto my couch. "Talk to me, man. What's going on?"

I shake my head. "I'm a mess. I don't know how to be this person, man. You can't understand what it's like."

He stares at me like I've said the stupidest thing in the world. "To fall in love with someone? It's the first time for me, too, bro, and I'm dealing with it." He lets out a heavy sigh. "You gotta have a real relationship with her, see if this is something you really want before you go acting rash. Until then, you need to stay away from her when she's working. Can you make me that promise?"

"I promise…I'll try and stay out of the round room."

Tyson gets up from the couch and starts for the door. "The ladies are off tomorrow, maybe then you could take things to the next level. Then, when you think of her having sex, it'll be you that pops into your mind. Trust me, it helps," he says and presses the button to leave. He suddenly has to sidestep. "Excuse me," he says.

I am surprised to see Ivory making her way through the door.

"Hey, babe," she says as she crosses the room with a grin on her face.

"What are you doing here?" I don't even attempt to hide my surprise.

"I arrived about an hour ago. One of the gals was telling me a rumor that you have lost your shit over one of the chambermaids. I had to come and make sure that things were okay with you."

"That's not what I mean and you know it. My private chambers are off limits."

Ivory ignores me, strides across the room, and takes a seat on my couch. I guess she's planning to stay a while.

She waves off my comment. Her near platinum hair is done up in deep waves. She certainly is beautiful, but nothing about her goes deeper than her spray tan. I've shared more with Tyson and Emmanuella than I ever have with Ivory.

"Please, if little Miss Brazil can sneak in here and roll around in your bed, then certainly I can, too. After all, I am your wife." She gives me a measured look, challenging me to say otherwise.

"Might I remind you that we are married in name only, a symbolic marriage is not legal. I only aimed to grant you a higher station when you walked The Chamber halls, but I can see now that I might have been mistaken."

"Oh, Mason. Don't be that way. Sit with me." She pats the couch.

I glance back between her and the door, pressing my lips together. "Ivory. It is time for you to leave. You seem to believe that you are above my rules, but let me remind you, you're not."

She stands up and gives a look like I just slapped her. "So that's it? She gets to come here and spend time with you, and I don't? In all my time here, I've never seen your private chamber, and she's been here a whole minute and what? You're replacing me?"

I roll my eyes and walk over to the door. "I never said any such thing. Those words came from your mouth. If you'd like to talk more, we can meet in my regular chamber. Later."

In a huff she storms toward the door. "I think I'd rather not. Call me when you've come to your senses. I don't plan on fighting for your affections."

"That works, too," I say and close the door the second she walks through it.

I walk over to my bar and pour myself a whiskey. Ivory got the wrong message about us. That might be my fault. But how could she believe that she was so valuable to me when I fuck everything that moves? Relationships are not my expertise, but, even I know that sex can't be the only reason to be with someone. That is all she and I have ever shared.

8

SAPPHIRE, THE CHAMBER

*M*aybe Mason changed his mind about wanting more. It's been a whole week and I haven't so much as passed him in the halls. My guess is that he freaked himself out, considering he stormed into my chamber while I was fucking Serge. I get it, there is no way he's amassed so much in his life by daring to care about someone other than himself. I could see it in his wild eyes, he was out of control, he wanted to get me as far from this place as possible. People like us don't ever give that much of ourselves. Vulnerable ain't sexy.

Still, I miss him. I hope he's just busy and I'm all wrong about his absence.

The kitchen is fragrant with bacon, biscuits, and eggs when I walk in. I find Flame and Sunshine at the table.

"Look who slept in," Flame says, pouring juice into her glass.

I rub my eyes. "I could hardly sleep with all this break-fasting going on. You fools are way too dressed and ready to start the day." I take a seat in my usual spot and load my plate with fruit, eggs and bacon.

"Why aren't you?" Sunshine asks. "We're all planning on spending a relaxing day at the spa. You should march yourself back to your room, throw on something, and come with us."

"Yeah, everybody else is already downstairs," Flame says.

I sigh. "Maybe," I say around a mouthful of sweet red grapes.

"What's wrong?" Sunshine asks.

My eyes tear with the thought of all of my problems. I wipe them away.

"Is it Mason?" Flame asks.

Of course she knows, she's in a relationship with Tyson, and he's the closest thing to a friend for Mason. I nod, fearing a full breakdown if I speak.

They both rub my back.

"Well, if it helps Tyson said he is really into you. He hasn't had sex with anyone other than you in over a month."

I laugh, but it's mixed with my tears, so it doesn't sound right. "He hasn't had sex with me, either."

They stare back at me, shocked.

"But…I thought you guys…I mean, you've been spending a lot of time together, and the two of you are the most sex-crazed people on the planet," Flame says.

"I know," I whine.

"You know what that means," Sunshine says.

"What?" I ask.

"It means he likes you more than we thought. Maybe he even loves you."

If only. "Am I crazy for wanting more with him?"

They both nod and laugh.

"I hate you both. Go get a massage or something, before I choke you."

"Are you gonna come down? You can't stay up here and sulk. We might even go to the pool and have the skylights opened. Come on. We need to do some normal stuff in this crazy-ass place," Flame pleads.

I nod. "Okay, let me finish eating and I'll throw on something and meet you guys down there."

They hug me and dash out of the room.

What a mess. How did I get myself tangled up with Mason? He is a genius, but he might also be insane. What does that make me?

I down a glass of juice and rush through my meal. This place just got way too quiet, and my thoughts are screaming at me. I throw on a blue romper, slip on a pair of sandals, and head out. After a walk down a long stone corridor, I get into the elevator. When I get to the spa level, I stupidly step out without looking to see if someone was waiting to enter the elevator. I bump into the one person I don't want to see.

"Ivory," I say.

"Sapphire, just the lady I was looking for. I was on my way up to see you."

I step around her and keep walking, if she wants to talk to me, she'll have to move in step with me. I don't have to guess what her visit is about.

"You think you're special?" she asks.

"Of course I do. Don't you think you are?" I say, not bothering to look at her and walk to the check-in counter for the spa.

"You know what I mean, missy. Mason is mine and you need to back the fuck off."

I exchange pleasantries with Roxy and take the robe that she offers me. I exhale and turn to Ivory for the first time, hoping that she gets the hint that she is boring me to fucking death. "Jealousy doesn't suit you. That shade of green really makes you look ill."

I turn away from her and make my way into the spa, leaving her dumbfounded.

"He will get tired of fucking a little tramp like you," she yells after me. "It'll take a lot more than sex to win over a man like Mason."

Bitch. I stop in my tracks. Expletives, both Portuguese and

English, flood my mind. This woman is trying to come at me with no idea of who I am or what my past is all about. I've been called so much worse than "tramp," sometimes by my own parents. She is going to have to grab a thesaurus and come up with something a bit more original, but I know exactly how to shut her up. I am about to break her shit down. Of course, she thinks Mason and I have been fucking, who wouldn't? Hell, even I was surprised that he waited until he got me alone before deciding to practice some restraint, but that is the strange and complicated truth.

For her, it is the only weapon I wield to shut her the fuck up. I turn around and take slow steps to her, closing the distance between us. I have to look up at her in her silvery red-bottomed stilettos. I'm a good four inches below her in my flat sandals. I fix my eyes on her and meet her death glare. Then I smile.

"I'll bet you'll find it surprising that he and I haven't had sex. Not once."

Her mouth drops open, knowing what that could possibly mean. Of course, she doesn't know that he hasn't spent time with me in a week, but that's okay.

"Never underestimate a tramp like me." I widen my smile. "Oh, e feche a boca antes de pegar uma mosca," I hit her with one of my avó's Portuguese sayings, warning her to close her mouth before she catches a fly, then walk away.

After my run-in with Ivory, a day at the spa with my sisters is just what I need to forget the stupid sneer on her face when she called me a tramp. For good measure, I even erase the mental image of her mouth open in shock that maybe I'm not the competition. It might just be there is no competition, I may be the victor. But with Mr. Mercurial at the helm, how could she or I know where we stand?

I decide to relax and enjoy a restful afternoon and clear my mind of all of it, *including* Mason.

9

SAPPHIRE, THE CHAMBER

*W*hen I arrive at Mason's private chamber I find it empty. I thank Tyson for letting me in and decide to take a seat to wait for him. There is some amount of excitement in not knowing when I'll be summoned, but it is heavily laced with the frustration of being left in the dark. It's been almost two weeks. He'd said he wanted to date me, but I guess he left out the part where he tells me how often. I miss him much more than I thought I would.

I didn't know how to dress for our date, so I opted for simplicity, choosing a deep electric blue mini dress and silvery-blue heels with straps. I used to like the color, but in the months that I've been here I am growing to dislike it very much. I get the whole idea of creating this magical sex world where we all embody our characters, but if I was running this show, I would limit the donning of the selected colors to the nights spent inside of the actual chambers rather than every fucking item of clothing provided being in the same shades. Seeing us all together is seriously absurd, we make up quite the rainbow. But, it's not my show to run.

The minutes tick by. Ten, then twenty, then forty-five.

When I realize he isn't coming, I stand to leave. Just then, the door slides open and there he is. My heart's rhythm picks up and my skin is warm and covered with goosebumps just looking at him.

He's wearing an untucked white, long-sleeved shirt, fitted enough to show me the goods, a loosened black tie, slim-fit dress pants, and his thick, dark hair is unruly. *Is he fucking kidding me?* How am I supposed to resist him when he looks like a star billionaire exec in an erotic porno? *He's so damn fuckable.*

We stare at each other across the room. Mason just looks like a wealthy tycoon of some sort of industry. The sort that would be seen aboard a yacht or on his private jet. His confidence oozes a good three feet ahead of him and his charm rivals that.

"Sorry for my tardiness. We had trouble with one of the lottery winners."

My mind immediately thinks about my sisters. It was almost forever ago that Serge bruised Flame up, but for some reason he is the first thought I have when I think about trouble with a lottery winner.

He closes the distance between us and uses his finger to smooth out the crease between my eyebrows. "It's nothing like where your mind is going. One of the guys had some issues with transportation and we needed to send the jet to retrieve him. He went on and on over the phone, instead of just getting to the point. And worse, he would only speak with me. Did I keep you waiting long?"

I exhale the breath I was holding. "Nope, I was getting ready to leave because I figured you were tied up. Running this place must be time-consuming. That must be why it's taken so long for us to see each other again."

His face is grim at hearing my words. "Can I make you a drink?"

"Sure, anything."

I follow him to the small bar and watch him mix and pour and shake until a pretty blue drink is sitting in front of me.

"I call it the 'Sapphire.' It just so happens to be my new favorite."

Hmm. Favorite? That sounds like the flavor of the month. Not exactly what I was going for, at least not anymore. If I want him to want more with me I need to change his perception, while seeming only more than slightly interested. I take a seat on a stool and sip the drink named after me.

"It's good. Thank you."

He pours himself one, and in the corniest of actions, raises his glass to clink it to mine. I close my eyes and push back the sarcastic thoughts swirling around in my head. *Are you an inner dork? This is super cheesy. You know that, right? Just fuck me already.* I manage to politely nod in recognition of his toast.

"Emmanuella," he says around a sigh.

"Yes, August?"

He lets out a breath and takes a drink.

I have just about had enough of the cloak and dagger with him. I don't like games, and he is making me crazy.

"This is all wonderful Mas—"

His hand comes up, but I correct myself before he can get the words out.

I smile. "August. But what are we doing here? We are not these people who slow dance into a relationship. What do you want from me?"

He looks at me over his glass as he takes a long draw of the special blue drink. I can't read his expression. He sets his glass down and we lock eyes.

His face moves closer to mine. I don't move. When his wet lips graze mine, a moan escapes me. But he breaks the contact almost immediately. One chaste kiss, leaving my lips burning, my stomach in knots, my skin tingling, and my heart racing. *Damn.*

"When I was six, I asked my parents for a puppy, and they said no." He takes steps toward no apparent destination, maybe just to gain some space from me. He stops and turns back to me.

"So I asked them for a sibling, they said no again. I took another tactic and just asked for some friends to play with." His face has fallen and his eyes are lost in the memory.

"Didn't you have school friends?"

He shakes his head. "I didn't have a traditional education. I was educated by private tutors. We traveled too much for me to attend a regular school; the tutors were able to go with us as we visited every continent. It didn't matter to my parents that I was lonely."

"That sounds awful. Did your parents play with you?"

He scoffs. "Alice and Montgomery Mitchell? Ha, they treated me more like a possession than a child—something that existed and needed to be dealt with, not loved or adored. I always thought growing up that I would have a bunch of kids and give them all the love I missed out on," he ends on a small laugh.

My heart wrenches for him. "You still want a bunch of children?"

He shrugs. "Haven't really thought about that since I was a boy. Seems so far away now. I gave up on wanting things that matter—you know, love, relationships, and family." He breaks eye contact and stares at the floor. "I never thought those things were ever for me before."

"Before what?" I ask.

His eyes find mine again and hold on. "You."

My cheeks warm. He wants a relationship with me. Or at least he can see himself in one with me. That is promising.

"What about you? How do you feel about relationships?"

I take a sip of my blue drink and think about his question.

"I don't know. I never saw myself in a relationship before. But if I did have kids I wouldn't raise them the way I was raised."

He closes the distance between us and laces his fingers through mine. "Tell me all about it."

I stare down at our entwined fingers and my soul smiles. How can such a simple action carry so much meaning for me?

"Here's the short version. Strong Brazilian Catholic parents have three daughters. The oldest and the youngest are perfect and as pure as the sun, and the middle child must have gotten all of the sex hormones from the other two in addition to her own. She regularly disgraces the family with stories of her sexual exploits and is labeled the family slut, skank, and hoe. Oh, and let's not forget damned." I look down, fighting the tears, but they fall anyway. It has taken me years to get used to the way my family sees me; the fact that they don't accept me for who I am if I can't be like them and it just...hurts.

His fingers caress my chin and he lifts my face to his. His lips kiss my tears and his tongue is slow and purposeful as he licks near my mouth. I bring my hands behind his head and thread my fingers through his hair. I'm cautious, not wanting to scare him off, but my pussy is hot and wet with want. My breath is slowly growing faster, but I refrain from dominating this moment that he's created.

When he pulls away from me I am bereft. The cold that settles inside of me makes me shiver.

He climbs onto the stool next to mine. "Fuck parents and their expectations. And fuck them more for forcing their weird shit on their kids."

I nod.

We sit in silence, the weight of the conversation heavy upon us.

"Do you think you would have turned out differently if they didn't raise you and a normal family did instead?" I ask.

He shrugs. "I think so. You?"

I shake my head. "I think I would have made the same choices about sex, but with understanding parents, I probably would have avoided some risky behavior. Then again, maybe not. I don't regret who I am, they do."

"I'm glad." His face is grim when he looks at me again.

"Sometimes you look at me like you hate me," I say.

He laughs, but doesn't answer. Instead he downs his drink, gets down from the stool and helps me off of mine. I don't ask where we are going, I just follow him. I think I might follow him anywhere. We cross the room and head in the direction of his bed and with each step closer my pussy wets with anticipation. *Yes, finally.*

Mason guides me to sit on the edge of his bed. He backs away from me, his dark eyes hooded and assessing. He licks his full lips and watches me.

I stare.

My lord. He unbuttons his shirt with deliberate slowness. I lick my trembling lips as I watch. I pull my legs together and squeeze, or my pussy might just detach itself from my body and gobble him up. I envision my hands caressing his strong pecs and pinching the nipples. His shirt hangs open on his arms and I want to take the bumpy ride down his tight stomach. *Fuck yeah.* My eyes travel lower. His cock pushes and strains against his pants. I gulp and swallow.

When my eyes travel back up to his, his smile is devilish, tugging at one corner of his mouth. He knows he is the shit, there is no denying that. My heartbeat is clouding my hearing. I don't move, not one inch. Mason pulls his pants down and steps out of them. He is wearing small, blue briefs. *My chamber blue.*

I smile and wonder if his color choice has anything to do with me.

"Do you know how much you frustrate me? Every day I regret bringing you here. I should have known the day I saw you that you would ruin me. I don't hate you, Emmanuella. I stare at you that way because of what my feelings for you make me want. It scares the fuck out of me, and I should send you away right now."

His chest rises and falls as he stares at me.

"Well that was *mean* and *sweet*."

"It's the truth." His face grows grim and frustrated again. "What would you have me do? Give all of this up for love?" He paces.

I jump at the words. "You love me?"

He stops pacing and lets out a heavy sigh, like he is letting go of the burdens of the world. "How the fuck am I supposed to know what this is? I have never been in love or been loved, for that matter. All I know is that if I fuck you I think it'll be over for me. You will be mine. No one has ever been mine before, not even my parents. I'm scared, Emmanuella. Of you." He is out of breath.

I stand up. I believe he might be mine, too, if I treat him right. He is so much more delicate than I imagined. I have to wonder if I am the only person who has seen this side of him —the human beneath the monster everyone sees his as. I'm not a stranger to his way of life. Hiding feelings is something that I have become an expert at. Referring to myself the way the world sees me—as a slut—to soften the blow before someone else tries to treat me that way.

August is less sure of himself. When he is August, he strips away his armor, revealing something sweeter and softer—vulnerability. August could never captain this vessel. It's more than just keeping his name out of the mouths of others. This business is not a legal one, but these monikers give us more than anonymity. It's like I told the other girls, "Separate yourself from all that you are in your soul and become this character for the sake of your own sanity." And now I see he does the same by protecting his inner softness under his tough shell. It is as brilliant as it is sad. For me, it is another reason to fall. The trust he has given me is priceless.

My dress is only attached by ties at the shoulder and with two swift movements I stand before him in my jewel-toned matching bra and panties.

His breath catches in his throat. His eyes are pained, like seeing me this way is breaking him in two.

"August, you scare the shit out of me, too." My breaths

are shallow. "You control everything here. I hold no cards—" My throat tightens on the words. His eyes don't leave mine. "I think about you nearly every fucking second of the day. When I'm in my chamber it's you I imagine. You can send me home anytime you want or not summon me at all. You can choose to fuck me or not fuck me and I'll still hold my breath waiting for you to call on me. I want to spend any amount of time with you, and I pray that you'll want me enough to let me stay, because I am falling in love with you." My breaths are as heavy as if I just ran a mile.

I watch as he brings his hands to his face. One at a time, he removes contact lenses and turns to set them into a container on a side table. He turns back to me with striking blue eyes. His face is softened, somehow. *Him*. It's the real him that he shows no one else, he is giving this gift to me.

"You are the most beautiful man I have ever seen."

His response is a shy laugh that causes my heart to swell in my chest.

He moves to me and pushes me toward the bed. I sit down. He soon drops to his knees. Then, his lips are on my lips, my cheeks and the hollow of my neck. The contact leaves me faint and dizzy. I moan softly.

His breath is hot on my skin causing it to sizzle. His lips move to the crest of my breast. He pulls one of my bra cups to the side, freeing my nipple from its struggle against the fabric. My head falls back as his tongue dances around my nipple before latching on and sucking.

"August, oh my…. I can't breathe."

His laughter vibrates against my tender skin.

"Fuck," I say and bite my lip.

His lips move on much too soon, and he starts planting soft kisses on my stomach.

"Ahh, I can't take this." No one has ever…*taken their time with me.*

His hand presses against the fabric of my panties. He must feel how hot my pussy is. I hold my breath in anticipation. When I look down he is looking up at me with a wicked smile on his face. He pulls the panties aside and slips an unknown amount of fingers inside of me.

My hips lift from the bed on their own accord. "August, August," I breathe his name.

When he pulls his fingers out, I long for their return. He reaches for my panties and pulls them down with care. I shiver as air hits my flesh. First his tongue, then his lips taste me.

"Yes. Finally, yes. This is what I want."

His mouth latches on to my clit and he sucks with the lips of an expert until I am jerking, shaking, and shuddering. Tears leak from my eyes onto his bed.

Breathless, I thank him.

He rises and pulls his bottoms off. His cock is everything I remember from my first night here. It's long and thick and pointed upward slightly. *Rare.* It's just what I like. I might lose consciousness. I unclasp my bra and toss it to the side. We stare at each other in our barest forms.

"Lay down," he commands softly.

I do as instructed, my body shaking and weak. He positions himself over me. "I love you, Emmanuella," he says with an intense gaze. Then he plunges inside of me.

Stunned, I am silent. My brain can't comprehend the words he just uttered because his cock is hitting me in that sweet spot. He locks eyes with mine—another first—as he rocks inside of me, steadily in and out, in and out. My eyes flutter and roll back in my head as tingly electricity shoots through me.

He moans heavily as he pushes deep inside and rolls his hips in slow, delicious circles. I grab onto his ass, pulling him closer, deeper. Holding on for life.

His cock swells against my walls as he moves faster and faster, harder and deeper still. With each push and roll I am carving space in my heart for him, crashing and falling into the unknown sea of love. My only hope is that I don't drown as I come apart. Fiery sensations rock my body, and he follows close behind.

Still inside of me, he gives me a sweet kiss, before pulling his cock out and falling onto his side.

I lay still, unsure of what to do next. Will he want me to get dressed and leave? Just because he professed love to me doesn't mean he meant it. Lust and passion do weird things to the mind.

He answers my unspoken questions when he pulls me into his side and wraps his arms around me, kissing my neck and shoulders.

Could it be true?

We lay in silence. I'm enjoying the splendor of *new*.

"I love you, too," I say, breaking the silence.

His only answer is to pull me closer, holding on so tight I fear to hope he may never let me go again.

10

SAPPHIRE, THE CHAMBER

*W*hen I roll out of bed, I am full of both hope and worry. With each month that comes and goes my anxiety grows. The clock is ticking on my fairy tale and I am struggling. Mason is seamless in his ability to be August when we are alone and Mason when we are not, adding to the rumor that I am his Chamber Seven plaything and nothing else.

The rumor mill also spilled the beans that Ivory is back in the building and in poor spirits. I want to know if Mason's and Ivory's relationship has changed since he and I professed our love to each other, but doubt that it is my place to ask. After all, I regularly have sex with seven different men a night, I clearly don't have the right to request exclusivity from him. Granted, at the eight-month mark, even things inside my chamber have changed, and not all of my visitors even want to have sex anymore. Some just want to spend a couple of hours in the company of a woman whose sole purpose is to listen to them and hang on their every word, and, sure, there is some cock sucking and other sex play, but not as much as before. When I first started to notice the decline, I thought Mason had meddled and asked them to be more hands off, but my girls report the same type of atmosphere inside of their chambers.

All of that doesn't even matter. My reality is that in less than two months, this chamber will be ending and everyone will be sent home. I just don't want to be included.

It's my last night in the Chamber before my scheduled days off. Living this way is like straddling the line of two distinct worlds. My days off belong to August and I can't wait to be in his arms tonight, but first I have seven lucky bastards to deal with.

"Hey, Flame," I say when I walk past her in our shared bathroom. I close the stall door. I do not wake well, and mid-day naps have always been the worst for me. Still, we all learned early on that we have to take them in order to have enough energy for the demands of our chambers. I'd say me more than them, because I often share my time between my chamber and Mason.

"You good?" Flame asks.

"Yeah, worn out. You?"

"Same. Ready to be done with this place and go home. I miss my family so much."

I don't respond. I think about going home and it's the last place I want to be. I do miss my sister, though. She must think I'm dead by now. "Yeah, I do miss my family, but I don't want to go home. You know that."

Her sigh is drowned out by me flushing the toilet. When I open the stall she is brushing her long, dark hair. I join her at the counter.

"How is Dominic?" I ask, using his real name.

Her smile is megawatt. "He's amazing and wonderful, but on to the more important question. How is Mason?" She winks at me.

"Mason is...wonderful and amazing and frustrating and worrisome."

She turns to me and gives me a look that says she feels for

me. "Do you think he is really going to send us home?" She asks me.

I laugh softly. "I know for a fact that he will. That's the part that scares me."

She wraps me into a big sisterly hug. "He won't make you leave. I keep the things I know about the two of you under tight wraps, because Dominic probably shouldn't be confiding in me. But I know for a fact that Mason is head over heels for you."

A couple of tears spring forth from my eyes. When we part, she gives me a sympathetic smile. "You got this. Just keep doing whatever you're doing and he'll never let you go."

I sigh. "I hope you're right. I can't go back home. I've told you what it's like there."

She lets out a breath and turns back to the mirror. "Well, I think we're all fucked when we go home…at least a little bit. Who would believe this? We can't tell them much and no one will understand why we just stayed here. We didn't fight or protest, we just gave in and let this happen to us."

I push her and suck my tongue at her. "Bitch, please. You are strong as hell, we all are. We chose to protect the people we love. We are on a big fucking island in another country, I'm sure. Where were we supposed to go with guards around? Sucking dick while eating the best food and living in plush digs isn't 'slumming it.'"

"That's not fair, Sapp. You wanted to stay the first day you got here. Some of us had our first sexual experiences in this crazy-ass place, and here I am standing next to you like it's nothing."

I raise my arms at her and look at her like she is insane. "We are human. You had two choices: adapt or curl up and die. I think you all staying and following through means that you're some bass-ass bitches."

She stares at me, but I can see her wheels spinning and

she laughs. "'Bad-ass bitches?'" She hip bumps me. "I like that a lot. I love you, sis."

"I love you, too. Now shut the fuck up so I can go eat. I have a busy night tonight."

She rolls her eyes at me and I scoot out of the bathroom.

～

FIVE HOURS LATER, I am sitting across from a lottery winner—my last for the evening. Runner is his chosen name. He is a sweet man; around fifty years old, I would guess. He has deep brown skin, brown eyes with flecks of honey gold, and a thick accent suggesting he is from the Caribbean. I can't remember the last time we actually had sex. I think the frequency is too much for him. So instead we partake in one of his favorite activities, strip chess. At this point in the game, we are both naked.

"You know, this game can go on for hours."

He looks up at me. "I know that."

"But you don't have hours," I remind him.

He smiles and a quick breath escapes him. "This I also know."

I return the smile and check his king.

His face is puzzled as he figures out a move. I watch as he successfully rescues his king and gets him out of harm's way.

"Dang it!" I say.

He sits back in his seat and regards me.

"You really are a beautiful woman, Sapphire. What will you do when you leave this place?"

I pause from my move and look at him. I shrug.

"Oh, come on. You have to know. The time is drawing near."

His words cause my heart to ache and my belly to flip-flop.

"Yeah, I know. I'm not sure the choice is mine."

"You're speaking of our curator. I had heard rumors of

something between the two of you." He continues to stare at me, like he is studying me. I look away, not wanting to squirm under his stare.

"A word of caution, my dear?" he asks.

I shrug and look up at him. "I'm listening."

"You are young and beautiful." He looks down at the chess set. "And, remarkably smart. Don't be so quick to hitch your wagon to a man who can create a place such as this. When broken hearts heal, it is usually with a battery of scars. I don't want that for you."

His concern is sweet. "Thank you, Runner. I appreciate your concern, but I am more like him than you might think. And I have nothing to return to when I leave here."

He scoffs. "Preposterous. You have the whole world. And if you need a familiar face to help ease your transition, might I suggest my country, it is beautiful ten months out of the year and you would love it there. My home is on a private island, with servants, beach bungalows, trees baring the sweetest fruits...every amenity." He smiles at me while I contemplate his suggestion of me joining him when I leave this place.

"Are you suggesting that we..." I point back and forth between us.

He shrugs. "I make no assumptions. Time will tell. You are special to me, Sapphire. I would like to explore...possibilities with you."

I bite my lip and lean back in my seat. "Thank you for the offer. I will keep that in mind, Runner."

His smile is broad and his eyes light up, filled with what can only be described as hope. "That's all I ask."

I lean forward. "One more thing."

"What's that?"

I move my piece. "Check and mate!"

11

SAPPHIRE, THE CHAMBER

*R*unner's kiss on the cheek leaves my face warm. Not because I have feelings for him, because I don't. It seems love is in the air all over this crazy place. Sweet things are happening all around me. Sunshine has a lottery winner that has fallen hard for her and so does Sky. They used to be shy and afraid. Now I see their strength unfurling itself and breaking through.

I make my way to my bathroom to get cleaned up. I have exactly thirty minutes before I am to meet August in his room.

"You're bath is ready for you," Reza says, passing me. "Do you need anything else?"

"I don't think so, thank you for everything," I say and give her a hug.

I turn to walk away, when I hear her greet August.

"Mr. Mason. Can I help you?" she says.

He smiles at her. Before his eyes find mine. "I am fine, Reza. Just came to see my girl."

"Well, good night." She scoots off, leaving us alone. I'm naked, my chest rising and falling in only the way it does around him. His eyes are covered with the brown contact lenses that change the way he comes across. Not because brown is bad. I have brown eyes. I think it's because they weren't the eyes he was born with.

"What are you doing here?" I ask.

He steps closer to me. "Are you not happy to see me?" He is close enough to reach out and touch me, but doesn't. His expression hard to read. *Is he upset with me?*

"Of course not. I was just getting ready to wash up and come to your room."

I turn to the bathroom, leaving him in the center of my chamber. Already undressed, I sink into my bath. It is hot just like I like it, and I close my eyes and melt into the water.

The sound of the chair scooting against the floor alerts me to his presence. I don't open my eyes. I clear my head of everything, including him. Especially him, because he is being weird right now. Moments later, he is still silent.

With my eyes closed I speak to him. "Are you going to sit and stare at me or are you going to tell me what your problem is? Because I can hear your breathing is weird."

He laughs, but it sounds off, causing me to open my eyes and look at him. There is anger bubbling under the surface with him, I can tell.

"What, August? Just spit it out, for fuck sake."

He deadpans. "You'll 'keep that in mind?'"

What is he talking about? Then realization hits me.

I roll my eyes. "I thought we agreed that you wouldn't watch my feeds anymore because they make you crazy." I start washing up.

He crosses his arms over his chest. "Well, not watching was making me even crazier."

I scoff. "That's hard to believe."

A small smile breaks through the grimace. "Still doesn't answer my question."

"Really? He's a sweet old man. What was I supposed to say? Wasn't it you that took a few million dollars from him for a fantasy? Kicking him to the curb would be the opposite of that."

"You have a point. But fifty is not that old. Are you sure he isn't what you want?" He already looks like he hates my answer and I haven't said shit.

I stare at him like he has three heads. "I won't dignify that question with an answer. I'll let my actions over the past couple of months answer the question for you." I stand up and grab the nearest towel. It is plush and soft, and warmed, thanks to Reza. I wrap it around myself and he extends his hand out to assist me from the tub.

"Thank you."

He smiles down at me. "Sorry. I'm not very good at this."

"No, you're not. I'm gonna tell you the same thing I told your *wife*. That shade of green doesn't suit you. I'm yours, we've already established that."

He holds his hands up and follows me around the large bathroom while I dress. He looks more like a lost puppy than the man who rose from the floor the first night.

I turn abruptly and poke him in the stomach. His hard muscles tense. "Stop watching my feeds."

He wraps his arms around me and scoops me off the ground. "I promise I will never watch again." He kisses and bites my exposed skin on my neck and shoulders, causing me to squeal.

"August, I'm getting dressed. I have a date with a sensitive egomaniac!" I squeal.

"Oh, yeah?" He bites and licks me, freeing one hand to tickle me, sending me into fits of laughter.

I poke more. "Did I mention he is green with jealousy? Even though *he* is already married and *I* should be the one who is jealous?"

He halts and sets me down. He is bristling.

Shit. I went too far.

He stares down at me. "I haven't touched Ivory in months."

"You haven't?" The words come out with a breath. My skin warms and tingles.

He steps closer to me. "And might I say that *that* particular shade of pink on your skin agrees with you." He bends down and brings his lips to mine. I close my eyes waiting for them. They are equal parts gentle, wet, and hot. I let out a moan into his mouth. Nothing is better than this.

I pull back and look up at him. "Thank you, it's a new color that I'm trying," I say.

He brings his lips back to mine, this time, tasting me. The sensation travels down my throat, chest and stomach, before pooling between my legs.

"Ivory and I are not legally married." His breath warms my skin.

I swallow the growing lump in my throat. "That's good to know. So—" I swallow again. So much energy is coursing through me and my heartbeat whooshes in my ears. "Are we going to your room now?"

He shakes his head and turns toward my chamber. He offers his hand and I take it. Once we are in the middle of my chamber he stops.

"I am done with images of you in this fucking place. I need to create my own memories. Starting with that." He points to my pony.

I break out into a smile. "Oh, you mean August?" I slip out of my clothes and make my way to my pleasure pony. A thought comes to me. "What about the guard downstairs?

He shakes his head. "He isn't downstairs anymore. I sent him away."

Hmm. "I like the sound of you inside of my chamber. It'll help me too." I twist a dildo onto the backside of the pony, depress the lube button and watch the glistening gel, fall down the sides. "You, right here." I point to a spot with the best view.

He rushes to the spot I pointed to.

"You named your pony after me?"

A small laugh escapes me. "Anything in this room that brings me pleasure has that name. All I want is you," I say and sink down onto the shaft. The material that it is made of is different than most, and it feels like the real thing, with warmth. I stare at him as I roll my hips on the shaft, my head falling back. I pinch my nipples and grind the cock hard. For extra, I push the button that makes the pony rise and fall, just like on a merry-go-round. I suck my finger, pretending it's him, moaning and staring down at him through hooded eyes. He stares back at me like I am something he has never seen before.

I summon him with my finger and he slips out of his clothes. He steps onto the pony, placing his feet onto perfectly placed pegs that puts his cock at sucking height.

He holds onto his shaft until I latch on. He tastes like romance and lust and sex and love. I suck it with reverence and possession, like the very first night, while I grind on the cock deep inside me. When I come, I press down on the cock and ride it out, my energy on him in my mouth. With my tongue, I swirl around and around and take him deep into my mouth until he is overcome, and I don't spill a drop.

He lifts me off the horse and is buried deep inside of me before we reach the bed. I can't get my mouth open wide enough. I want to devour his mouth, his entire face. I am overcome with more than I can handle. Our pace is that of forbidden lovers with only moments before they will be separated forever.

Before we get to the bed I stop him and guide him to my sex chair. I need his body against mine the entire time. We fall onto the chair clumsily, our mouths desperate for each other. Our breathing is heavy and our loud, guttural moans serve as a soundtrack. I wrap my arms around him and press him into me, my heart swells when he does the same. I love this man. I show him with every bounce onto his length, with every roll and buck of my hips. I squeeze the walls of pussy around him like a vice. He grabs my ass and pulls me onto him, pushing himself in more.

"I'm coming, August. I'm fucking coming so hard! I fucking love you so much." Tears spill from my eyes. He pulls my lips to his and joins me. Our bodies rock and shake as one, squeezing each other hard enough to break something. I will never know anything like this again in this life.

"I love you," he says into my mouth over and over.

We collapse back in the chair.

When I wake, we haven't moved from our spot. He is still deep inside of me, I am against his chest.

"Morning...I think?" I say.

He pulls his watch to his face and has to rub his eyes to see clearly. "Why, yes it is."

I unfold from him and pull off of him. My body is sore from last night and from sleeping in a chair.

12

SAPPHIRE, THE CHAMBER

*R*eza shaking me is a shock. She has never entered my chamber while I busy myself with a lucky bastard. I have to separate myself from Hunter's cock and wipe my mouth. She has our attention, and, judging from her expression, something is wrong. Hunter and I remove our earbuds. That's his kink. We wear them while we do it on the bed, in the swing, or with me restrained. His feed is my voice talking dirty and my feed is his. He was just repeating how he wants me to fuck him with my dirty mouth when Reza interrupted.

"What's going on?" I ask.

She twists her hands. "I'm pretty sure I just heard a gunshot."

Impossible! Here? "I didn't hear anything." I hold up the earbuds and Hunter and I stand.

She paces. "It was distinct. A scream. A gunshot. And another scream."

The three of us look to the stairs as we hear a commotion, followed by light and hurried footsteps. Weaver appears at the entrance of my chamber. In a move that surprises me,

Hunter steps in front of me. My hair stands on end. There's only six weeks until the end of this year and only once has someone come running into my chamber—Mason.

One question is in the front of my brain. *Who did the screams belong to?*

"Come with me at once," Weaver says. "All of you."

Hunter and I throw on our clothes while my personal guard waits, his expression grim.

I expected him to march us down the entrance steps that he came up, but instead he leads us down the stairs that lead to my bedroom. I'm quiet as we pass the beds and stop inside the living room. Face upon face regards me with fear and concern. The room is crowded with groomers, guards, and lottery winners. One face isn't present among the sea of faces.

I turn to Weaver. "Where's Flame?"

He doesn't respond.

I search the room and find Zion, Flame's groomer and rush to her. Sunshine, Ivy, and Raven follow close at my heels.

"What happened? Where's Flame?" I note the blood on her fingers and clothing.

She breaks down. "I stepped away for five minutes. I went to gather fresh towels and by the time I got back..." She crumples to the floor.

"What happened to Flame?" Raven shouts. "Where did the blood come from? Is it Flame's?"

She nods and my heart sinks. My stomach knots up and I want to throw up.

"Is she...dead?" I ask and the room quiets on an inhale awaiting her answer. Judging her state the answer could be the last thing we want it to be. After nearly a year inside of the walls of this place, we've all grown closer, even with the men who started out as strangers. We all hold our breath awaiting her answer.

She shakes her head. "No, she's pretty bad, but not dead."

Air whooshes out of our lungs.

"And the gunshot?" A deep voice breaks into the thick air.

Raven and I assist Zion up from the floor and guide her to a chair. She grabs a pillow and squeezes it to herself and closes her eyes to any further questions.

Weaver clears his throat. "Flame is okay. She's been taken to the infirmary. We are still investigating what happened and will provide information as we get it."

Two hours later we learn that Serge, wanting revenge for getting his ass handed to him, decided to attack Flame. He planned to kill her, Mason, and Tyson. Serge was killed by Tyson.

The men are released back to wherever it is that they go, while the six of us dress quickly to go and see Flame.

13

MASON, THE CHAMBER

*T*he shit has hit the proverbial fan. A lottery winner is dead and a chambermaid is in the infirmary. In all my years of operation, this has never happened. It's my fault, I lost focus. Tyson is on his way to meet with me and it is not going to be pretty.

I pour myself a double scotch on the rocks and down it just as the door opens.

"Boss." Tyson stares at me, grim and worried.

"Please have a seat." I gesture to the stool near mine.

"If it's okay with you I'll stand," he says.

I nod. He really is a beast of a man. "Very well." I spin on the stool to face him. "This is a shit show," I say. "There needs to be some sort of action of the punitive variety taken."

"I don't see why the fuck so. I'm security, and I did what security is supposed to do. I took care of the problem."

I'm down from my stool. "You fucking killed a man, Dominic!" I yell, calling him by his real name.

His anger rolls off of him and hits me in the chest. "And he was planning to do the same to you, me, and Flame!" His chest is rising and falling fast, his breath's heavy. "It's your fault. You know that, right?"

I scowl at him. "How is that?" But I already know the answer.

"Do I have to spell it out to you?" You dropped the fucking ball while you were so distracted with Sapphire. I told you to send his ass packing months ago. He creeped all the woman out and then he went and roughed up Vivian. Instead of eighty-sixing him, you piss him off by beating the shit out of him. You dropped the fucking ball, Mason. You were right, you don't get to be in a relationship and run this place." He stares daggers at me.

"And you do?"

He lets out a long breath. "Probably not, but I'm not in charge here."

"I'm sending you home today." I let out a breath. "Immediately, in fact. You'll have time to say goodbye. You've upset the order of things here, and frankly, the other lottery winners are worried about security and the fact that you shot one of them." I pause. "Flame stays here." I brace myself for his possible attack.

"You can't do this shit to me, Mason. What the fuck am I supposed to do, just leave her here with you, and..." He gestures everywhere at once. "...and them?" He is fuming. If he were a cartoon, I imagine he'd have steam coming out of his ears and he'd be five shades of deep red.

"Why now?" he continues. "It's been six weeks since this shit went down. I did what you said and I've kept my distance from Flame. I can keep everything under control. Besides, the rest of the lottery winners are not a problem."

"You're right. They are not the problem. Like I said before, you are. A man is dead because of you."

He gets in my face. "It was self-fucking-defense and you know it! We'd all be dead if I didn't act!"

"Because you went and fell in love with a Chambermaid," I huff. I do my best to keep my calm. I step away from him, leaving him rooted in place, seething. "I would have dealt with him. Now there is a death that needs explaining. That needs to be covered up." I turn to him. "This is why I hate guns in my chambers."

"What about you and Sapphire? You bear no fault here?"

I shrug. Inwardly, guilt sours my stomach. "The same rules don't apply to me. I always take a lover. You are not permitted to do the same for a reason. Look what happened. You risked our whole way of life because of her, and now I have to send you home." I return to the bar and pour another drink.

"Of course, I will pay you for the entire year. Another four million in your account should have you sitting on quite a nest egg. You have an hour to gather your shit."

He calms down with each visible inhale and exhale. "What about Vivian? I want to take her with me."

"No."

He stares me down. Any friendship that we might have had is dissolving before my eyes; hate fills his eyes.

"What if I take you out then walk out of here with her?"

I laugh. Guards are inside this room with me right now, and more wait for him outside. "You don't think I thought of that very thing the moment I decided you would leave here without her?"

The sound of weapons cocking echo throughout the room.

"If I die, you die. It's as simple as that."

He ponders his new situation.

"So, you expect me to leave her here alone?"

I roll my eyes. "She won't be alone. You may hate me now, but I consider you a friend and I will make sure that she is taken care of and released as scheduled. If you do anything to jeopardize that, there will be unfortunate consequences." I close my eyes, regretting this. He really has come to be my friend and banishing him will leave a hole, but I wasn't lying when I told him the other lottery winners have muttered concern, and this is my business. I know for a fact things would not have escalated to a death if he was not in love with the woman he was protecting. My decision is final.

Tyson doesn't make a verbal threat, but his expression makes my heart stutter. He turns to leave without another word. I believe he just became my enemy.

14

SAPPHIRE, THE CHAMBER

*I*n our final weeks, a lot has changed within the walls of The Chamber. For one, after the death of Serge, Mason kicked Tyson out. Now my girl is depressed and even Mason is less cheery than usual. Tonight is our last night. All the parties and festivities are over and we all face the anticipation of tomorrow. Though, I am hoping for a much different outcome than the other girls are.

I'm already home.

Mason and I have a date tonight. It's his last chance to give us both what we want—a chance at forever.

~

"YOU LOOK LOVELY TONIGHT," he says staring at the deep plunge of my sparkling blue gown.

I smile at him. "This old thing? Just something I found in the back of my closet."

We pick up our glasses and clink them together.

The liquid has to compete with the lump growing in my throat. I haven't seen as much of him as I would have liked in the last few weeks. With the dismissal of his most trusted employee, he has had to take on additional roles, and, of course, I understand. The problem for me is the missed time together hasn't given me much time to work my magic.

Logic tells me I should keep quiet and see where this little dance leads, but, frankly, I have run out of time. "So, tomorrow—" I let the word drag and hang.

He exhales and runs his finger around the base of his glass.

"It came pretty quick. You will be a very rich young lady tomorrow. Any ideas about what you'll do next?" he asks.

And there is my answer. My throat thickens with tears I will not allow my body to shed, not here in front of him. I am not enough for him, that much is clear. I look down at the table to collect myself. I only look up when he clears his throat.

He reaches a hand out to mine on the table, but I slide it away before he can make contact. I don't think he gets it.

"Emmanuella, I'm not the guy who gets the happy ending. Do you honestly think I deserve one?" He stares at me with sad eyes.

I nod and he responds by shaking his head.

He scoffs. "You don't get it. I'm the bad guy."

I shrug. "I'm not exactly perfect. I thought we'd get to be imperfect together."

He sits back in his seat and regards me with a near smile tugging at his lips, but his eyes are so sad and, suddenly, so far away.

My stomach dips and clenches, because I know what this is.

"Hmph. Maybe in another lifetime..."

A traitorous tear slips past the rim of my eye and I swat at it quickly. "Then I guess this is the goodbye that I feared." I push back from the table. There is no way that I can sit across from him and play make-believe tonight, not when I know that he is planning to send me home tomorrow. My heart aches and I press my hand against my chest to offer much needed pressure.

"Wait, you're leaving? I thought we could say a proper goodbye." His eyes are big and he gestures toward the bed. *And there it is.* I am what Ivory said I was to him, a plaything. Sure, I might have been a favorite, but, still, a thing to pass the time nonetheless. I was a fool to believe a man like him was capable of giving me anything more than that. I hug myself and walk toward the door. I'd run if I thought my legs would let me, but a weight has set in and they are leaden as I walk. I turn toward the entrance and find him only a couple of feet behind me. He really is a beautiful man. I was duped with his "call me August," blue eyes, and promises of love. *Fuck, I'm gonna miss him.* I turn and offer him a tight smile and answer his question.

"Sorry, but I think that," I gesture to the bed, "means something different for me than it does for you." A sob rips through me and I cough in an attempt to cover it, failing miserably. "Thank you for being so good to me while I was here. You might not believe it, but I think you have a lot of good inside of you. I wish you could see that."

I close the space between us and plant a kiss on his cheek and walk out the door.

Worrying that he might follow I run, my legs heavy, but sure. Tears blind my path, but I have faith that it is clear and that any person who sees me will give me easy passage by stepping aside. A hole is tearing through my chest and the once warm center is cold and barren. When I have traveled far enough, I collapse onto my knees and let go, until I am empty and dry.

15

SAPPHIRE, THE CHAMBER

"*You* okay?" Flame asks.

I shrug. "I mean, I will be. Right?"

She looks around. "Let me see. Kidnapped, wild sex with strangers, falling love with the man in charge, and four million dollars in the bank?"

I laugh. "You forgot, beaten up by one of the strangers and witnessing a shooting."

She shakes her head and laughs. "Oh, we're talking about me? I thought we were talking about you."

A heaviness fills the room. "Did we forget, 'heart broken by the man in charge?'"

She bites her lip. "Yeah… I guess it serves us right, falling in love with the men of The Chamber. Why didn't we just serve our sentences like the others without romantic entanglements?"

I stuff some toiletries in the small overnight bag that was provided for us. "Yeah, and where would the fun have been in that?"

"You are so right. I was going to ask—"

"Sapphire, I was hoping to find you here," A familiar,

unwelcome voice interrupts us. I look up to find Ivory looking fresh. Her platinum hair is done up in a high ponytail, and she's wearing a white blouse, navy skinny jeans, and her signature stilettos.

I raise my eyes and then roll them in Flame's direction, an action that I know Ivory saw and I don't care one bit.

"Hey, I'm gonna run and grab something from the kitchen," Flame says and scurries off before I can stop her.

I turn to Ivory. *May as well get this over with.* "What can I help you with, Ivory?"

She smiles and it is full of gloat and satisfaction. "I just wanted to see you off." She walks around me like a cat trying to keep its distance. "Mason is busy making plans for our vacation. You see, we always spend some time in a relaxing place for a few months before the next Chamber begins. Usually, Tyson joins us, but seeing how he isn't here anymore, it'll just be me and Mason. I can't wait." She claps her hands.

I zero my attention on stuffing my bag full. There is no way she gets to see me cry like a love-stricken fool.

"Seems like you were a plaything after all. Sure, he delayed the gratification, but sometimes the rules of the game must change to keep things, *exciting.* I wonder who his toy will be in the next cycle?" She widens her eyes in wonder.

"Great. You won. He's all yours. Can you please leave now? I have packing to do so I can get out of your hair."

She comes up behind me and squeezes my shoulders. I shrug her off of me and she laughs. "I'll let you get back to packing. I'm sure your plane will be here soon."

She makes her way toward my room door.

"Hey, Ivory?"

She turns.

"I hope your pussy dries up and falls off."

She scoffs. "I'll just bet you do." She taps the space above it and walks away.

Flame returns seconds later.

"What the hell was that all about?" she asks.

"I hate her and she came to rub it in my face that I'm going home." I throw my arms up. "Oh, and she and fucking Mason are going on some lavish vacation." I ball my hands into fists and then I use my middle fingers to gesture to the door she left from.

"Wow, whatever I did, I'm sorry," Raven says, walking in.

I wave her comment away. "Not intended for you," I say.

"Oh, I know. I saw Princess Platinum coming from your room looking smug. You know, you can kick her ass before you leave. I can help you." She does some crazy martial arts kick-punch combination and lands in a fighting stance.

"That would make my year. But honestly, I just wanna get out of here," I say. *I won't cry, not for him.* We fall into a three-person hug that turns into four when Sky joins us.

I am going to miss these ladies more than I thought.

An hour later, I am being ushered outside the same way I came here—with a hood over my head. In a way, it's better because I might break if I looked into the faces of everyone and didn't find the only one I want to see. I'll never find my way back here.

I have to believe he thought he was going to keep me at some point and changed his mind along the way. Otherwise, why reveal his real name and those damn blue eyes? Even knowing that isn't enough as I glide across the skies...home.

16

MASON, THE CHAMBER

*T*oday is moving day. One by one, this years' Chambermaids will be jetting off to reunite with their loved ones. Emmanuella and I said our awkward good-byes last night. I hated breaking her heart. But in time, she'll thank me for letting her go. I am not the man for her, or anyone, for that matter.

I temporarily lost my mind letting things get as far as they did, anyway. Hope is like a fucked-up magical being or something. It really sweeps in, lightens your heart, and feeds your soul something sweet and tasty. I fell hard for hope.

I have been running Chambers for ten years now. In those ten years, I have grown fond of plenty of girls. I remember the very first year of The Chamber when I met Silver. She was strong, gorgeous, sexual. She became an instant favorite. I took her from jolly old England. She resisted this life at first but eventually acclimated to it. She spent many nights with me. I wanted to keep her, but thought better of it. After all, it was the very first year.

It went like that year after year. I always found one. Year Two there was Onyx. I took her from the Ivory Coast. She was sensual, with the softest, deepest ebony skin I'd ever seen. During that year, I couldn't get enough of her.

Over and over I found a favorite. I found Genesis in England, too. Gorgeous. But for some reason, I never felt the desire to subject her to The Chamber.

Her story was awful. Worse than mine.

She wasn't like the others who had families. She had no one; she was all alone. I felt like an uncle or a father to her. Which struck me as weird, because being caring and loving is not in my DNA. I brought her into The Chamber to save her from the streets. She is still with me as a groomer.

It wasn't until Year Five that I met Ivory, and I did keep her. I took her from Illinois. It just felt right. We tell everyone that we are married, and we are, but not legally. I wanted her to feel power within The Chamber's walls, and nothing gave her more power than being the master's wife.

I make it my business to pick girls from all over the world because it makes it a lot harder to make connections from kidnapping to kidnapping, and, ultimately, to me. I operate under absolute secrecy.

Rule Number 1—
No one uses their real name in The Chamber.
Rule Number 2—
I pay my employees and the captured handsomely to show my upmost appreciation.
Rule Number 3—The girls are to be treated like princesses.
Rule Number 4—Keep moving.

From the obscure to the opulent, I run my Chambers all over the world. Discretion is used when selecting the men who will be chosen to participate. These men pay millions of dollars each to participate. I hire the most talented employees, from guards to computer geeks, in order to keep The Chamber running smoothly without detection.

I am a successful businessman, with a net worth in the

billions. I don't do love and romance. I don't fall in love with Chambermaids. The ones I take a liking to are merely pets. I observe them for two years before we snatch and grab. My security team and I know what they like, don't like, and who their friends and enemies are. We learn their daily routines down to how many times they wake up in the middle of the night to pee.

I personify control. Nothing and no one ruffles my feathers.

So now, after ten years of control over everything in my world, I find myself up shit creek without a fucking paddle or directions home.

I have been Mason to everyone who encounters me, until Emmanuella Maria Alves got a hold of me. Under her dark, seductive gaze, I became August Mitchell again...for her. She stripped me down to the barest parts of me. I gave her my truth, I gave her me. I loved being August with her. I didn't even want to hide myself, because for the first time in my life someone loved *me*.

I could see it. I could feel it. The scariest part is, I craved it.

Every time she touched me I became more him and less me. She never feared me. From the first moment I laid eyes on her, I knew I was in trouble. In ten years, not one woman ever wanted to know the real me. I never once lay in bed and *just talked* to anyone in my life. Sex has always been rough, dirty, and sometimes angry for me. But not with Emmanuella. With her, each and every time was special.

She was different. I was taken aback by her curiosity about me, her tenderness. At first, my hackles raised. I thought she was trying to find a weakness to help her escape. But I saw an innocence behind her eyes. She really wanted to get to know me. I don't know why I trusted her, I just did. I wanted to share my story with her, and it felt good...until it didn't.

I melted into a puddle and spilled my entire life story, feeling more human by the day. Every moment I was with her, I was becoming August. With mere words, she catapulted me back to that insecure teenage boy in search of love and acceptance.

I'm sure my parents must have loved me in their own way. Whatever I wanted, I got—everything except their attention. I was raised by my nanny, whose ass I was tapping by the time I was sixteen. I was happy in my little world. I never felt a loss for anything. I only knew the type of love my parents gave me. They taught me that everything and everyone had a price and that to be loved was less important than to be respected and feared.

My jet-setting parents didn't have time to raise me themselves. They were more concerned with building the family's fortune into something astronomical than worrying about some damn kid. And since that was the only life I knew, it seemed perfectly fine by me. I didn't know until Emmanuella came into my life what I missed out on growing up.

So to say I was caught off guard by her affection for me would be stating the obvious. I fell in love with her. During her year here, I felt like we were in a real relationship. Though, I'm not sure that I know what a real relationship is.

I began to understand how Tyson felt about Flame. I hated kicking him out. He was the closest thing I ever had to a friend. He will never know that I did it as a favor to him so that he would be free of The Chamber. Free to love.

If I'd never met Emmanuella, I know that I would have never thought about who Tyson fucking loved to make a move like that.

She changed me.

So I did right by Tyson, even though he will never know my motives. People only respect power. I did something so out of character for me because he was loyal and deserved that much from me—that, and the seven million I gave him. The only person who knows the real reason I kicked him out is Emmanuella. In fact, she knew my reasons before I did, because she saw right through me. The hold she had on me was frightening, and nothing frightens me.

That is why I had to let her go. Being the coward I am, I didn't even say goodbye to her. If I would have seen her, I wouldn't have been strong enough. She is mine and I want only her. But this love shit is making

me weak. It's turning me into a fucking pansy who wants everyone to be fucking happy while they run around singing fucking love songs. I can't run this place feeling like a silly, giddy fool. I swear, I feel like baking a fucking cake or cookies after spending any amount of time in Emmanuella's presence.

I had to make a choice. I'm the monster. At least that is the nickname one of the other Chambermaids gave me. The monster does not play well with others.

~

"Sɪʀ, you told me to let you know when Ms. Sapphire was ready to go."

I nod. "Thank you, Weaver," I say, making my way to the car. I'm three cars back from the sedan she is traveling in. The private airstrip isn't that far from us. My heart aches as I climb into the sedan. I fist my hands in the seat and wait for the driver to climb behind the wheel. It would take nothing for me to jump out and rush to her car to pull her into my arms. I could hear her call me August again at least one more time. Maybe forever.

"You got room for one more?" Ivory asks, but doesn't wait for permission. She slides into the back seat with me.

"I can't wait for vacation. Where are we going this year?" she asks with excitement, but I don't look her way or respond. My heart is in my throat; I don't think I could speak if I even wanted to.

I watch them help her out of the sedan. She turns her head

this way and that because her vision obscured. It's a punch to the chest and throat.

"You are making the right decision to let her go, Mason," Ivory says and tries to lace her fingers with mine, but I pull away from her. My eyes never leave Emmanuella as she walks up the steps of the plane. My eyes sting with tears. I squeeze them shut and take in a few breaths. I try to telepathically tell her that I love her. I wish I was strong enough to make her mine. But she deserves so much more than me.

Maybe I could have kept her on as an employee. Sure, we couldn't be together, but at least she wouldn't have had to return home to a place that she never belonged. She confided that to me and I'm sending her back to them. She must hate me.

I faked her out and gave her hope, too. Many nights we spoke of a future together. She probably feels so betrayed by me. *Fuck.*

I want nothing more than to bring her back. We belong together. I will never know tenderness like she showed me. She was the perfect blend of sweet and sexy that I will never find in my life again.

As the plane taxies down the runway, I panic and reach for the door. The things that she told me about her family and how they made her feel about her sexuality...she doesn't deserve that. She is a goddess. My goddess. I have to stop her.

I reach for the door handle.

"Mason, please, let her go. If you really thought she should stay she'd be here with you right now. There must be some reason she's on that plane."

I don't tell her that all of those reasons have nothing to do with Emmanuella and everything to do with me. There is no way that I can be the man and the monster, and I let her go because I am afraid of who I will become if I let the man take over.

17

EMANNUELLA, NEW JERSEY

*W*hen I step off the plane in New Jersey, I want to cry. Maybe I will take my Chamber earnings and open up a Chamber of my own, or just disappear. Going home is a bad idea. But no matter how

embarrassed my family is by me, it would be awful for them to think I'm dead. So I climb down the private plane's steps reluctantly, to begin my journey to my family's house. I can't even call it "home" anymore. In fact, I know that I left my home the moment I left The Chamber.

As promised, there is a limousine waiting for me when I step off the plane. The driver opens the door for me, and I slide inside. I hope that it takes forever to get to East Brunswick.

Maybe I shouldn't go back at all. I could give them a courtesy call. I have four million dollars in the bank, thanks to the gracious gift that Mason bestowed upon us. My fellow Chambermaids think of it as hush money, but I think of it as payment for a job well-done. What Mason doesn't know is that for him I would have done it for free.

I'm glad that I have it, though, because the money gives

me something I didn't have before—options. My family already thinks I'm missing, so if I don't go home, what would it really matter? I've been gone for a year, so any grief they suffered should be over, or at least the worst of it. I just can't face my parents giving me that look they always tried to mask. My year at The Chamber was a nice break from society and its judgements. It was an amazing feeling in The Chamber to never be on the receiving end of that look. I was a star in The Chamber. The girls always came to me for advice, from things as simple as how to give a blow job without gagging, to how to fake an orgasm. I guess they mistook my love of the place and confidence for expertise. Truth be told, it was both.

I remember back to the introduction night. I thought it was the classiest night of my life...

Mason went all out for us that night. His intention was to create a tasteful experience, and he did just that. The seven of were dressed in exquisite gowns.

Flame wore a beautiful crimson gown adorned with ruby jewels.

Violet had a gorgeous, soft lavender gown, with amethyst jewels.

Sunshine wore an enticing yellow gown, with canary diamonds.

Ivy looked like a princess with her emerald green gown and emerald jewels.

Sky's blue eyes dazzled in her sky blue gown and icy baby blue Swarovski jewels.

Raven looked lethal in her inky black gown and onyx jewels.

Then there was me. I wore a sapphire sheath, with deep sapphire jewels dripping from my neck and ears.

I remember every detail of this night because it was on the night of introductions that I learned that Mason was an artistic genius. What better way to describe how we were to be treated than to introduce us in such a tasteful manner?

Each of us looked more like princesses being introduced at a royal coming-of-age ball than what was really happening. He was accomplishing two very important tasks. The first was setting the standard. He made sure each lottery winner knew that we were important to him and that we were to be well-treated toys to be played with, but respected.

The second, I think, was to confuse us girls. In our year we were treated very well. There was only one incident with one of the girls and a lottery winner that got out of hand. But that was handled swiftly.

No dungeons, no starvation, no brutality. Only opulence, excess, beauty, and…lots of fucking.

Our groomers lined up next to us. Most of the groomers were giving the girls pep talks. Not me. My groomer, Levi, didn't have to say shit to me. I couldn't wait.

Mason supplied us with a lot of personal perks during the year. For starters, the place was a vast castle. We girls had access to the second and fifth floors. On those floors we were free to roam.

Our living quarters were on the fifth floor. The living space was huge. It reminded me of a sorority house. I shared a room with Flame and Sky. Of course, our areas of the room were color-coded with our Chamber colors, so mine was deep blue. We had access to a full spa, a gym, swimming pools, and groomers.

The groomers were entrusted with keeping us gorgeous and fuckable—Chamber-ready at all times. That included getting us ready sexually for each visitor. But for me that was never an issue because I was always ready. Especially when Mason finally sent for me.

That introduction night I gave Flame, Violet, and Sky a pep talk before we walked into the room full of lottery winners, who I referred to as "lucky bastards." I told them to "be" their colors, to use the tools that Mason had given them to their advantage. Let everything happen to their Chamber personas, not their true selves.

We were goddesses that night.

I only wished they would have embrace it, instead of shivering in fear.

When it was my turn to enter the room, I walked across the stage with pride. I owned my moment. I took my time crossing the stage. The lights were much too bright for me to make out any faces. It didn't matter, because the only face I wanted to see was Mason's. I think I loved him from the minute he rose from the floor, promising me a place in the world where I finally fit in.

We modeled for the lucky bastards that night in our fantastic gowns as vibrant young women. Then we were led to a changing room and stripped down to nothing except the jewels around our necks. We became pieces of art.

I had no idea what Mason planned for us, but whatever it was I would be game...

Like I said, I was a rock star. Sex was what The Chamber was all about, and sex is what I'm good at. I was happy to oblige all who came to my chamber, but six months into it, Mason changed the game. With his romantic walks on the grounds, private dinners, lovemaking, and holding hands in front of everyone, he planted seeds inside of me that grew and sprouted into hope and the possibility of more that I neither wanted nor expected.

We shared things I have never shared with anyone but my sister—my fears, hopes, and dreams. I laid it all before him, trusting that he would never close that door now that he'd pushed it open. He trusted me enough to tell me his real name and all about his past.

But I guess that didn't fucking matter, cause my ass still got sent home.

I am thankful for the money, even though I would gladly trade it all for Mason. Money can really be the great motivator. Without it, the only choice I would have is to tuck my tail between my legs and crawl home. With it, I can go wherever I want and do whatever I want. I know for a fact that I don't want to go home. And I am just about to tell the driver to take me to a hotel when one name pops into my head.

Gabriella. Damn it. My baby sister is the only one who ever understood me. She and I are by far the closest, and she never once judged me for being who I am. And I don't judge her for being a good girl. We are who we are, and we love each other. I need to go home so that she knows I'm alive. Then she can see me for herself, in the flesh. It is what I would want her to do for me if the tables were turned.

Of course, it takes the driver no time to pull up in front of my house. *Wonderfuckingful.* My stomach is a puddle in my socks as I gaze up at the two-story clapboard house with the brown shutters. It's a dwelling full of strangers, save for one.

"Can you give me a minute?" I ask the driver. I am in no hurry to walk up the sloped driveway. Once I do it's back to being Emmanuella again. Sure, Mason liked to call me by my given name when we were alone, but it meant something else when he did. It was his way of saying he really saw *me. Fuck.*

"Take all the time you need, miss," the driver replies.

Both of my parents' cars are in the driveway. *Great.* A true reunion. I guess it's now or never. I need to remember that I am returning here by choice, not because I have to be here. I have options. That thought steels me as I open the door. The driver hops out, unprepared for my sudden exit. I am already out of the limousine by the time he makes it around to me. "Thanks for the extra time," I say to him.

"Good luck to you, miss."

"Thank you. I'm going to need luck and more."

I don't look back, but I cringe when I hear the chauffeur drive away.

My escape.

Ringing the doorbell is the hardest thing I've ever had to do in my life so far. I am not sure that I can do this. I haven't been subjected to the feelings that the people beyond this door have about me for an entire year. Beyond this door I will be judged, always.

I have options.

This is my choice.

If it gets too hot in this fire, I can always find a cooler place.

I press the doorbell.

When the door swings open, I am face to face with my father. The expression on his face tells me that he is in complete shock. I'm sure that I am the last face he expected to see standing on the other side of the door. He looks the same. He has naturally tanned skin like mine. His hair is thinner than before, mostly white and bone straight. He's short and stout, but less stout than I remember. He takes me by surprise when he grabs me into a strong embrace. I am rarely on the receiving end of an embrace from my father. He isn't one to show much affection. Especially toward me.

"*Querido Senhor.* Emmanuella. Is it really you?" His strong Brazilian accent fills the entire entry.

"*Sim, Pãi.* It's me. I'm home."

"Maria! Gabriella! Marianna!" he yells. "Come now! Hurry!" He has excitement in his voice. At least I think it is excitement. It could be fear. With my father, who knows?

I hear the scamper of panicked feet as the rest of my family comes running. They probably haven't ever heard my father yell out in such a manner. He is usually very soft-spoken and reserved.

"Manny, what is it?" my mother asks with concern in her voice. Then her eyes find me. "*Querido Senhor!* Emmanuella!" She crashes into my arms, as do both of my sisters.

I never expected such a reception, my family crying in joy to see me.

"Let her sit. Please," my mother says, fussing over me, and pulling me into the house. Which is difficult with my sisters still entangling me in an embrace. I take a seat with one sister on each side of me, and my father on the smaller sofa across from me.

My younger sister and I could almost pass for twins. My

older sister looks like us, but she takes more after our mother's side of the family. They never release me.

"What happened? I saw them put you in the van!" Gabriella shrieks. "I tried to chase after you, but I couldn't keep up. You were gone. I thought you were dead."

My mother comes back with a silver platter of tea. Tea is her answer to most of life's problems. Well, tea *and* church.

"Please, Emmanuella, tell us where you have been for a year," my father says.

My mother busies herself pouring tea into Avó's china. She hasn't changed much in the past year. My mother has always been gorgeous. Beauty-pageant gorgeous. She is very fair-skinned, with long, light brown hair, taller than my father and model thin. She hides her beauty because of her strict religious beliefs. But I have seen pictures of her when she was my age, she was stunning. I would like to think that the three of us all received our fair share of the best of our parents. My younger sister and I have naturally sun-kissed skin year-round. We all inherited our mother's thinner figure, with some

extra curves from our father's side. Gabriella and I are darker-haired like our father, while Marianna has lighter hair like our mother.

I take a sip of my tea. I really don't know what to say. The love my family is doling out right now feels so wonderful. For the first time in forever they look concerned for me, rather than embarrassed and ashamed.

"Well, I'm sure Gabriella told you most of it. That night, we were just having fun. I went out to get some fresh air, and a van pulled up in front of me. It was right out of a horror movie. I didn't have a second to react. The van doors flew open and there were three men inside. A fourth guy put a white cloth to my face and shoved me in. That was it. When I woke up I was on a plane. I tried to fight, but they drugged me again, and the next time I woke up I was in a castle. I have no idea where. We were not allowed to leave the castle the entire time we were there."

"We?" Marianna asks.

All eyes are on me.

"Yes. We. There were six other girls there. All taken like me."

"Why? For what reason would someone do this?" my father asks.

"To make us sex slaves, *Pãi*," I say flatly. *Let's get to the point.*

"I'm calling the police." My father jumps up, and his face is angry and afraid.

"And tell them what, *Pãi*? That I'm home? Okay, then what? We were released, but we were told that if we said anything our families would be in danger. So call them, *Pãi*. Tell them I'm home, but that's it. I don't even know where I was for a year!"

Gabriella squeezes me tight. "You are so lucky. You could have been killed."

"She is right, Manny. We don't need this. Let us be thankful to God that our girl is home. No one needs to know what she has been through."

That is code for my mother not wanting to bring shame to our family.

"We will let her sleep a bit and then we will go to church and give our thanks," my mother adds.

I follow Gabriella to our shared room. I need to get some rest, or at least a mental break. My side of the room has not changed —a twin bed, a patterned quilt with abstract pictures on the wall. I fall into my bed. It is nothing compared to my luxurious beds in The Chamber. There was nothing regular and normal in that place, which suits me, because there is nothing regular and normal about me. I don't belong here in this place. This is not home. This is the place where my family lives. This is their home.

"You okay?" my sister asks me.

"I guess."

"Mom and Dad were really scared and crazed with worry about you. All of us were."

"I know."

"Of course they thought you brought this on yourself because you have always been so 'sexual,'" she says, doing air quotes. "They think that it is something evil inside you. You know how they get. Mom said she had an aunt that you remind her of."

I smirk at the thought. "I'm sure this aunt of hers was her least favorite."

Gabriella picks up her favorite stuffed animal, Rufus the Pig, and hugs it. "She didn't say, but I wouldn't doubt it. I really had to convince them that it could have happened to anyone. It could have been me." She puts Rufus down, crosses the room, and sits with me. "You know this wasn't your fault, don't you?"

"I know." I bump her shoulder gently with mine. "Wanna hear something crazy?"

"Sure."

"You can never repeat this."

"I won't," she promises. "I cross my heart," she says, crossing her heart.

"The year I was gone was the best year of my life. I never felt more alive or more like myself. I wish I was back there, with him."

"Really? 'Him' who?" she asks me. Her face is shocked.

"Really. I wish I was there now. I missed you guys, especially you. But I was a rock star there. 'Him' is Mason, and I am in love with him."

She flops back onto my bed and I follow her. She is the only family I know who I can share my secrets with. "Then I wish you were back there, too. I always hated how you were made to feel like the family outcast. You are my sister. I want you to be happy. Always."

"Thanks," I say, and we hug each other.

When I wake up a couple of hours later, my sister and I are still holding one another. I really missed her. We have always been close. She gets me and I get her. I wish I could take her with me—just the two of us. We'll see.

First things first. I have to deal with my parents, Marianna, and *church*.

18

*R*eunions are tiring. I am still not sure that I did the right thing by returning home, but at least my family knows I am alive. Gabriella and I excuse ourselves to our bedroom. All I want is to get into a bed and exhale this breath I've been holding.

"Are you sure you're okay?" my sister asks me when I close our bedroom door.

"Yeah."

"Dinner wasn't too bad, was it?"

"No. I mean, Pãi didn't stare at me like I had four heads. Just three."

We both laugh.

"Are you nervous about going to church?"

"No." I lie. "Do you think they know I'm not *actually* going to catch fire when I step onto hallowed ground?"

"Don't be silly. Of course they don't know that," she teases.

We burst into laughter.

"I just ask because I know you hate church more than I do," she says.

"True. I wanna get it over with. I don't see what good it's gonna do. But I'm going to behave myself and play along."

"Now that's the spirit."

An hour goes by and our parents have yet to walk upstairs to tell us it is time to go to church, and I sure as shit am not gonna go ask. So Gabriella and I spread out across my bed, watching reruns of sitcoms. I guess they changed their minds about church because we watch TV until we fall asleep.

My mother actually decided to let me sleep before forcing religion down my throat. *Wow.*

~

AS IT TURNS OUT, she was only biding her time. The next morning, right after we finish our breakfast of toast and juice, we are headed to Our Lady of East Brunswick. We meet with Father Brookmire in his office. This must be more serious than I thought. I have never been in a priest's office before. I had expected to light some candles in thanks for my safe return home. Really, the thought of anything more formal than that never crossed my mind.

I can tell from the way Father Brookmire gazes upon me that my mother filled him in on what she knows of my recent experiences. *Fucking fantabulous.* Just what I want—a priest to know about what happened to me.

"Please have a seat, Alves Family," he says to all of us.

Father Brookmire looks the part of a priest. He's got dark brown hair, a peaceful face, and a gentle spirit that is naturally calming. His appearance suggests he is doing what he was born to do.

"Emmanuella, it is a blessing that you are home safe. Your family was so worried about you. We all were."

I'll bet.

"Your mother and father tell me that you were forced to

do unspeakable things during your capture." He crosses his body in the sign of the Father, Son, and Holy Spirit.

I only nod. What makes my actions unspeakable is that I will never share them with the likes of him or anyone else in this room.

"We here at Our Lady would like to offer you a series of classes designed for victims of such crimes. We have also set up some special cleansing rituals that will help purify you at your parents' request. I would like to come to the house first thing in the morning to perform them. Is this okay with you, Alves Family?"

No, as a matter of fact it isn't okay.

"Yes, Father, of course," my father answers for all of us.

"I don't understand. *Why* am I being cleansed?" I am unable to wipe the disbelief from my face.

"Emmanuella, the Father is going to come over to purify your soul." My mother decides to add her two cents. "The reason this happened to you is because you have always had a darkness inside you, since you were a young child. We have always known it. This will protect you from something like this ever happening again. If we allow Father Brookmire to perform the cleansing, you can start over with a clean spirit, a new soul."

I stand up. *This is lunacy.* "Are you insane? Not everybody is born to be a nun or a saint, *Mãe*. There is nothing wrong with my soul. Some of the girls who were taken were as innocent as Gabriella or Marianna, or you! And, newsflash, you keep the soul you're born with 'til you die! You can't just get a new one! I'm pretty certain it doesn't work that way!" I huff.

"Dear, this is for your own good," my father says. He walks toward me and touches holy water to my head.

"*Pãi*, are you crazy? I'm not possessed! I was kidnapped!" I snatch away from my father. "Thank you, Father, but no thank you. Let's go!"

I burst through the office doors, and bolt down the church

aisle for the safety of the outdoors. What kind of people are they? I get kidnapped off the street—well, beach. I was minding my own damn business, and somehow this is my fault. They think because I like sex that anything that happens to me is my own making. *Ha!* "Ha!" I turn and shout toward the church. I walk toward the street. By now my family and the priest are standing outside. "So if I walk out into the middle of the street and get hit by a car, it happened because I'm evil inside, not because I'm just stupid?" I yell. I stand in the middle of the street. "Look, *Pãi!* I'm still alive!"

"Emmanuella Maria Alves, get out of the street at once!" my father shouts.

I am in tears. This can't be my life. "I'm not evil. I was just born into the wrong family," I say as I walk back to the safety of the sidewalk. I don't look at anyone. I just make my way to our parked car. My family follows me, apologizing to Father Brookmire repeatedly, like this is also my fault. They are the ones who thought this was a good idea.

I hear my mother telling the priest that we will see him in the morning.

Fat chance.

The ride home is brutal. Not one single word is spoken. I've been home one full day and already I am the cause of all my family's woes. I'm sure they liked it better when I was gone. Well guess what, so did I.

Two things happen when we get back home. The police show up to get my statement. When I tell them that I was taken by plane with a hood over my head, never saw the light of day for an entire year, and only saw the sky for the first time when I was released, they tell me how lucky I am to be alive. They leave after giving me their card in case I remember anything else. *Don't hold your breath.* Like I would tell them anything.

The second thing that happens is that my mother starts lighting her candles and incense all over the damn house. *Oh my fucking goodness, I have got to get out of here before the priest arrives in the morning.*

I scribble a note to my sister in the middle of the night after I know everyone has long gone to sleep.

Dear Gabriella,

I am so sorry to leave you before I can even get settled back home. But you have to understand why I can't stay. You have always been the only one to understand me, anyway. Pãi and Mãe really think something is wrong with me because I am not like them. I can't live in a house with cleansings and priests and sideways glances. The good news is, I don't have to. I will call you when I get where I am going. Right now I don't even know where that is. Tell Pãi and Mãe that I am sorry that I could never be the daughter they wanted, but at least they have you and
Marianna.

I love you and I will talk to you soon.
Love, Emmanuella

I HAVE no idea where I plan on going tonight. All I know is that I can't be here in the morning. I set the letter on top of her night stand. She will tell my parents that I left this time on my own. Maybe she will even let them read the letter.

I walk out the front door and I don't look back. All I have with me are the clothes on my back and my small purse. I told the rideshare to pick me up about a block from my house, just in case. The driver is prompt. When I slide in I say hello and squeeze my eyes shut. I've already arranged to be dropped off at the nearest suitable hotel. I just need a place where I can sleep for the night and figure out this shit that has become my life.

We arrive at the Doubletree. Fortunately, I can pay for it with my new bank card that came in a large envelope from

Mason. He thought of everything, including making our millions readily accessible to us.

After I check in to a swanky suite, I take my room key and munch on the amazing chocolate chip cookies they have in the lobby on my way to my room. I have a few things I need to take care of first thing in the morning. A new smartphone is definitely on that list. I also decide to change my name legally to Sapphire Emmanuel. I don't know how long the process is supposed to take, but I hope that if I explain my circumstances and pay well, I can shorten it.

Tonight I begin the process of reclaiming my true self. It took me twenty-two years to find her, but thanks to The Chamber, I know who I am, and I will not let anyone ever make me feel ashamed again. I am ready to embrace Sapphire completely.

I drift off, wondering how I will find Mason.

~

THE MORNING FINDS me in good spirits because I have a plan. By now, the priest should be showing up at my parents' doorstep to find me not there. *Ha!* Maybe he can cleanse himself. Knowing my parents, they will probably perform the cleansing ritual on the house, just to cleanse it from my presence. And I'm the freak?

I order pancakes, sausage, and orange juice from room service. It is delicious. I call the front desk and ask for a car to pick me up in an hour. I don't have time for rideshares today. I have work to do. I want out of this city ASAP.

The sedan is waiting for me when I step out of the hotel. It's ten thirty in the morning, so everything is open. I hit the cell phone company first. My new smartphone is already charged and ready to go, complete with a new number.

Unfortunately, I have to put it in my old name for now. The next stop is the mall, because I can't wear the same clothes everyday. I am not in the mood to be picky, so I grab a few pairs of jeans, some blouses, t-shirts, a light jacket, sneak-ers, flats, a pair of boots, and bras and panties. I also grab a small suitcase that can hold everything. My last stop in the mall is a salon. There, I pick up shampoo and conditioner. The driver loads everything into the trunk and takes me to the county building, our final destination. There I fill out the name change form, but I don't turn it in. Instead I ask to speak to a supervisor.

"May I help you, miss?" the supervisor asks. She looks reasonable enough. Probably a mother herself. Surely she will be able to understand my plea.

"Hi. I am here to get a name change. But I was reading the form and it mentioned publishing it in the paper?"

"Yes, that is standard."

"Well, you see, that would be the opposite of helpful for me. Uh, I was kidnapped and held captive for a year. You can Google it if you don't believe me. I was missing for a year and just released." Just in case she doesn't believe me, I Google myself on my new phone, and sure enough, it shows information about my kidnapping that made the news a year ago.

She gasps.

"So you see, it is important that my new identity is kept secret. Is there a way to speed up the process and keep it out of the paper?"

"Absolutely, miss. There are always special circumstances, and your safety is definitely one of them. I will file your form personally and mark it urgent and confidential. You should be Sapphire..." she reads my new name from the paper, and her eyebrow raises in question "...before the week is out."

"Thank you," I say rising out of my seat.

She extends her hand to me and I take it. "You are a very lucky girl."

"Yes, I know." But I am not agreeing for the same reason she means. I am lucky that Mason chose me. I am lucky that I had the honor of spending a year with him in The Chamber, and I need to find a way back to him.

I GRAB tampons and sanitary napkins from the drugstore, and some other necessities. When I get back to the room I order room service for lunch—a cheeseburger and fries. The front desk is happy when I tell them that I will be staying in the suite until next Tuesday. That gives four weekdays for my name change to take place. I don't want to book my plane tickets under my old name. Once it is complete, I will have to get a driver's license. But, shit, I don't even have an address. That presents a problem. I will have to use a fake address.

19

*B*risbane, Australia is the location of the next Chamber. It is a beautiful underground estate, complete with finished tunnels and pathways. Exactly what I prefer. I like my Chambers to make a statement. Some wealthy anchorite built it a couple hundred years ago. On the surface, it doesn't even exist.

The cost for a year rental is 2.4 million dollars. The owner believes me to be a successful, reclusive writer who is working on the next great American novel and needs the utmost seclusion.

The next group of girls have been selected, as have the lottery winners. The entire staff is on vacation. This is a much-needed ritual. After being cooped up inside for a year, we can all use a bit of sun and fun. I never tell anyone about the future locations until the last possible second. As far as I am concerned, *everyone* is on a need-to-know basis, including Ivory.

Two months. That is what everyone is allotted this time. Most who visit their loved ones explain their long absences by making them think they work on cruise ships or oil rigs. It seems to work just fine.

Ivory and I set out for Paris the day we sent the girls home. Last year, we vacationed in Oahu. The North Shore was restful. Paris will be the opposite. I like to switch it up.

Ivory left early this morning to shop with friends, which is great, because I need time to myself. I need time to think about my actions and to figure out how to get Emmanuella back. *Should* I get her back? Will I be able to operate as Mason, Chamber Master, when in the presence of her love I only want to be August Mitchell? I don't hate myself in her presence. I don't want to harm myself when she is around.

Right now, without her, in this hotel all alone, I have the strangest urge to throw myself out the window. No one knows this about me except Emmanuella. I have fought suicidal tendencies most of my life. I don't actually want to die. I only fantasize about ways to off myself. My imagination runs from the dramatic, like long-term self-poisoning, to a quick bullet to the head. Maybe it's for the best that she stays where she is, because she is a weakness for me. There is no room for weakness in my world. Besides, there is no room for both Emmanuella and Ivory.

With Ivory, there is no love between us, no weakness, only power.

I know what I need to help me think.

I walk over to the balcony and slide the door open. The air is fresh and cool. I gaze over Paris and its old-world charm before I hoist myself onto the railing. A simple breeze would be enough to throw me to my death. I know that is not my fate, because only the good die young. My head swirls as I realize how high up I am. I would probably die from a heart attack before I even made contact with the ground. The wind whips my long hair into a frenzy. I need a haircut.

I sit on the railing, my legs dangling below. I think about my life as it is now. Perfect. I *am* control, or at least I was before she came into my life. I can't even blame her, either, because I handpicked her. I should have known better. She gave me butterflies in my stomach when I watched her on camera. I have never felt anything stir within me before. But instead of running from the feeling, it only made me curious. It made me want her more. How do I choose between two such different paths? There is no way I get to have both. There is no such thing as a fairy-tale ending. And if they did exist, they wouldn't exist for me. I don't get the happy ending. I don't get to ride away on the white horse with the beautiful maiden. I don't even know why I even allowed myself to hope when I only deserve loneliness and an empty existence. Even now, knowing this truth about myself, I still can't help hoping.

Damn. I choose the happy ending. I knew it the second she boarded that fucking plane.

I need her back.

She is mine.

She is the one who changed me. She brought a pulse back into my veins and a beat back into my dead heart. Who wouldn't want to feel that way? In her presence, I believe I can be more. *Fuck*. She makes me a believer...in love...in the possibility of a happy ever after...in feeling something more important than power.

In Emmanuella's presence, I can be August.

I will speak to Ivory about my decision the second she returns from shopping. I know she will not be happy with the choice I have made.

I get off the ledge and head back inside. I need to see her. I rifle through my suitcase and pull out a thumb drive. It is the highlight reel of Emmanuella's stay at The Chamber that one of the computer guys made for me. I pop it into my laptop. The first day of The Chamber comes into view. The second I see her my dick aches. I miss slamming myself into her. I almost rip through my pants when she takes me into her mouth. I should have known that I would love her from that moment.

I set my erection free and begin stroking the shaft. With each stroke, she is with me. I am inside her, loving her, learning about her, and feeling her. Right now, all I can do is remember her. I grab some lube and watch our next meeting when she sinks down onto my dick, taking in my entire length.

I come yelling her name. Both of her names.

I fast-forward to the day when she tells me she loves me. She thought I was sleeping, but I wasn't. That was the most innocent and honest moment of my entire life—my girl lying across my chest professing her love for me. And I fucking let her go.

I come three more times watching us doing the most sensual, sexual acts to one another. No matter how many times I come, my dick aches to be inside her. Nothing else will stifle this ache except being inside Emmanuella's juicy walls.

When Ivory finally returns to the suite I am chomping at the bit. Eight hours is too fucking long to leave me alone with my thoughts. Seeing Emmanuella on the screen didn't help one bit. I need her more than ever now.

"How was shopping?" I ask her.

"Wonderful. I love Paris," she says, setting her plethora of bags down. "I need to fuck. You game?"

No. "Can we talk first?" To fuck her now would be cheating on Emmanuella. *What the fuck is wrong with me? I'll fuck anything. I'm losing my shit for this girl. Maybe she should stay where she is. She is changing me at my core and she is thousands of miles away.*

"Sure. What about?" she says, sitting. She removes her stilettos and immediately rubs her feet.

"I was thinking about bringing Sapphire back."

"Are you fucking serious, Mason? Why?" She stands up in protest.

"I want her."

"Fuck. I knew this shit was gonna happen the second that

little bitch put your dick in her mouth." She stares daggers at me for a full minute. "No. I refuse to share you any more than I already have to."

"What do you care? You're acting jealous, and she isn't a bitch!"

"This isn't about jealousy. You are mine. I don't do jealousy or love. I love to fuck, and I want you whenever I feel the need. I refuse to share you with some newer piece of ass. Now ram your cock inside me, and I promise I will erase her from your mind."

She gets up and strips out of her dress. She is completely naked. That would normally be enough.

"I'm not fucking you right now. We are talking, Ivory." I take a few steps back to keep some distance between us. "So, you hate her that badly? You refuse to share?"

In a bold move on her part, she closes the distance between us. She goes for my clothes. I am wearing track pants, so they come down easily. She grabs my cock in her hand and starts rubbing up and down the shaft. It feels awesome, but I only see Emmanuella. I don't see anything or anyone else. When she attempts to sink her lips around my cock I snatch back from her. She must think I am losing my fucking mind, and maybe I am. We are both in unprecedented territory.

"Oh my goodness, Mason. What the fuck is this about? Yes, I hate the bitch. Are you satisfied?" She is pissed.

I pull my pants back over my throbbing cock. "What made you think you would always be the only one? I am selective, but that doesn't mean you would never have to share." I stare at her before I continue. She is pushing me. I don't like to be pushed. "So you are saying it is you or her?" I ask.

"Yes."

"Fine."

"Fine?" she cocks her head to the side in question.

"Yes. You win." *It's her.*

"I knew you would see reason. We make a good team, you and I."

"I'm going for a walk," I say. I don't wait for her to say another word.

Her fate is sealed with a three-letter word. I close the door to our suite. Today is the last day for Ivory to be a part of The Chamber and my life. She just signed her resignation letter. I will make sure she is well taken care of because she was good to me. I don't make it much farther than the lobby.

I call my finance guy and have him open a bank account in Ivory's real name—Raimy Foster. I tell him to transfer fifteen million dollars into her account. That is three million for each year she was with me. I ask him to messenger the details of the transaction when it is complete.

The concierge is happy to accept the package and understands that it is confidential. I expect it by the end of the day. I head out of the hotel without looking back.

I love Paris. I'll bet Emmanuella has never been to Paris. I want to show her the world. I can see promise in the world if she is by my side. She makes all things possible.

The air is fresh. Unfortunately, before I go get my love back, I have to make a pit stop in L.A. One of my operatives says that he thinks our little Violet may not be strong enough to keep our secret. Business is business. I don't want to scare her. I just want her to remember that I have eyes everywhere.

I decide to visit my favorite café in Paris, Brûlerie de Belleville. The coffee is like nothing I have ever tasted. For the first time, I don't mind being alone with my thoughts. I sit back, people watch, and plan my future with Emmanuella. Will she want to be a part of The Chamber? I will give it all up for her if she doesn't. Will she want to get married and start a family? *Fuck. Me, a dad?* That shit doesn't sound right, but I will do it for her. Fuck, I wish I would've told her that I loved her the last day we were together.

It is crazy that in an instant I am looking at life through different eyes. I know now I can really see. Before I was blind.

20

*E*verything went smoothly. I am officially Sapphire Emmanuel. I know it kind of sounds like a stripper name. But it is who I am. I used my avó's address to get my new license. The only thing left to do is pick a city. I have always wanted to visit San Francisco and Las Vegas. I guess I will have to go with the one that has flights leaving in the next couple of hours, 'cause I want the fuck outta here.

After checking all of the flights leaving to both cities, it looks like I will be heading to San Francisco because they have a direct flight leaving sooner than the one to Vegas. I pack my suitcase and take a taxi to the airport.

I should probably get in touch with Flame, because her man and Mason have always been really close. I doubt that he would tell me anything, but he may be the best shot I have.

I am still in shock that he sent me home. I really thought he was capable of love. He showered me with tenderness. He told me about his past! He told me his real name! I'll bet nobody else knows that tidbit about him, even his precious fucking Ivory. From the moment he confided something so personal in me, I have dreamt of being Mrs. August Mitchell. It's crazy, I know. Deep down I always knew it was a silly dream. A man like that doesn't settle down with one woman. A man like that doesn't dream of that type of life. I mean, I don't want the whole "white picket fence with a swing set in the yard" life. In fact, I never imagined I would even have kids. I just wanted to be a part of his world and I wanted him to want me to be there.

Before I board the plane, I send Gabriella a text with my new phone number. I tell her where I am going, and where I will be staying. I also tell her that I will call her when I get settled. I don't have to tell her to keep this information from our parents. She knows if I am scuttling off in the middle of the night I don't want to be found. I never want her to worry about me again. She texts me back to "be safe."

I love my baby sister.

The flight to San Francisco is peaceful. The farther away from Jersey I get, the better I feel. I sleep most of the way. When we touch down, I say thanks to God as I always do after a safe flight. I might not be religious like my folks, but I know that it is more than engineering keeping my plane in the air.

The sedan I ordered takes me straight to the Ritz-Carlton. I am not used to being a millionaire, but thanks to Mason's high-end lifestyle, I'm starting to acclimate. It will still take some getting used to. The second my bags are situated in my room, I make my way out onto the streets of San Francisco. I ride the cable car from one end of the city to the other, hopping off at Fisherman's Wharf, Chinatown, and the San Francisco Botanical Garden. I even walk Lombard Street, which is a bitch.

By the time I make it back to my room, I am spent. I immediately go into the elaborate master bath and begin to fill the tub. My feet are killing me from exploring the city.

When the tub is sufficiently full of hot water and lavender bubble bath, I kick off my shoes and remove my clothes and step in. *Ahh.* This is what heaven must be like. I'm surrounded by opulence and beauty. My eyes close, and complete relaxation takes over.

I am so thankful to Mason—or August—for appropriating this life for me. I can take care of myself. I can stand on my own without my parents. It is the most liberating feeling in the world. The only thing I need to make my life perfect is him.

What would my life be like if we were together? Would I be the Queen of The Chamber? Would I be part of the selection process? Would he still be with all of the other girls? Of course he would. And he has Ivory. I can't expect him to give all that up for me. If my fantasy was reality, I would be there right now. No matter what role I have in his life, I have to find him. I would settle for just being a part of his world.

I dial the number that Flame—Vivian—gave me when we all went our separate ways.

She answers on the second ring. "Hello?"

"Hey, Vivian. It's me, Sapphire…Emmanuella."

"Oh my goodness. How are you?" Vivian asks me.

"I'm okay. How did things go with your family?" I ask her.

"It went as well as can be expected. They struggle with me keeping tight-lipped about the details. But I'm happy to be home. You?"

"Not so smooth. My parents tried to perform some religious cleansing rituals on me, so I bailed. I'm in San Francisco. Which brings me to my phone call. Have you been in touch with Tyson?" I assume she has. They were bound to end up together. I know love when I see it, and they were in love.

"His real name is Dominic," she corrects me. "He stopped by to see me, but he is giving me some space to figure things out. Why? Do you want to get in touch with him?"

"I want to go back, Vivian."

Silence.

I know she thinks I am insane.

"I'm more fit for life in The Chamber than anywhere else," I say.

"Hey, I'm not judging you. You were always more comfortable there than the rest of us," she says.

"Plus, I love him," I blurt out.

"Him who?"

"Mason."

"Wow, that's heavy. I can't really say I'm surprised. How about I text you Dominic's number? I don't know if he can help you. Remember, he didn't exactly leave on good terms. But I wish you all the luck."

"Thanks, girl. Good luck to you, too," I tell her.

"I hope Dominic can give you the answers you need. Call me anytime," Vivian says.

"Same, and thanks."

Hearing her voice felt better than I expected it to. She sounds good...happy. I know life inside The Chamber wasn't as wonderful for everyone as it was for me. If it wasn't for Dominic, I don't know if Vivian would have survived inside for an entire year.

I shoot a quick text to Dominic. He seems much more like a "Dominic" than a "Tyson." Everyone is in such a hurry to shed their Chamber pseudonyms.

Hi, Dominic. It's me, Sapphire. I was wondering if you have any idea how I might get in touch with Mason.

I don't expect a speedy response, so I return to my soak. My phone pings with an alert before I can close my eyes. I shake my hands to cast off any excess water.

Hey, Sapphire. Why on earth would you want to get in touch with Mason? You are a free woman.

It surprises me that he didn't know how I felt about Mason. I thought everyone knew. I wore my feelings for him on my sleeve.

I kind of fell in love with him. And it turns out that my own family is much less accepting of me. At least that is the feeling they gave me when they tried to perform an exorcism on me.

I wait for his response.

Damn, girl. That's fucked up. I will see what I can do, but Mason is only easy to find when he wants to be found. He's probably halfway around the world by now. But for you, I will see what I can do.

Thank you so much, Dominic.

Take care of yourself, Sapph.

Now that I have a real bloodhound on Mason's trail, I can relax in the bath. Tomorrow I will enjoy my new city.

~

SAN FRANCISCO IS everything I thought it would be. I love a city where I can feel the energy pulse through my veins. There isn't a "late for an important meeting" vibe here. Rather, there's a feeling of freedom and happiness. I can't stop smiling. I take in more sights and even hang out with some street performers. I've also learned that fresh seafood on the wharf is something everyone should experience.

When the sun begins to set, and I am completely exhausted from walking and jumping on and off cable cars, I head back to the hotel. I don't even make it to the bed. The couch is as far as I go because I barely have the strength to keep my eyes open. I flip on the television for background noise.

A sudden wave of nausea hits me and I hop off the couch and make a mad dash to the bathroom. I stay there until I hurl up everything I ate down on the wharf.

"Argh. Bad seafood." My head spins. I have to use the toilet for support to stand, because I need to get to the sink. I pull a hand towel from the rack and run cool water over it. It feels good on my face. *That's weird. I never get sick from food. I have an iron stomach.*

Then something hits me.

I haven't had my period or the shot. And I think I'm more than just a little late. *No. It can't be.*

I erase that thought from my mind. It has to be bad seafood, and maybe I am more stressed out than I thought I was. I have been through a lot in the last few days. It is just exhaustion, and suddenly I feel it—the weight of my life on my shoulders pulling me down. I shower and climb into my luxurious bed. I am asleep before I know it.

I dream.

I am back at my parents' house. It is my first day home. My family is so happy to see me. My mother showers me with love and adoration. My father gazes at me with pride and more love than I have ever seen in his eyes. We are a real family, and I am happy to be a part of it. The sunlight shining through the windows is cheerful and joyous. But just as quickly, dark, ominous clouds cover the sky and rain pours down. When I look back at my family, they are in black. Are they in mourning? My father is carrying a rope. My mother is crying and chanting something in Portuguese. Gabriella is crying, too, and she is repeating "no" over and over.

The priest appears. He is not alone. There are two large men with him. One of the men grabs me and forces me to sit down. My own father takes the ropes and binds me to the chair.

"Pãi, no! What are you doing?"

"Saving you, my child," he says.

"Please! No!" I scream out. I cry. I try to wiggle free of my bindings.

The priest begins speaking in a tongue I am not familiar with, and he dips his fingers into a dark, inky liquid and uses it to write symbols all over me. The men pour salt in a circle around my chair.

Over and over I scream to the top of my lungs.

When the front door blasts open from a massive force, everyone stops. I stop screaming, my mother stops chanting. We all stare at the open space for what seems forever. Then he appears in a shroud of light, just like the first time I laid eyes on him.

"August." I'm only able to whisper his name.

Two guards I recognize from The Chamber walk in carrying

large firearms beside him. "This is a travesty," August says, looking around the room. "I send her home to your care and this is how you treat her? You call yourselves family?"

One of the guards unbinds me. I run to August, folding myself into his welcome arms. "You saved me."

"I should have never let you go." He squeezes me, then looks at my family again. "You call yourselves saints? Look around. See what I see. You are no saints."

Gabriella runs to me and wraps her arms around me. "I don't blame you for leaving. I love you. I will miss you."

I hug my sister one more time and I walk out of the door hand in hand with August. And I don't look back.

∾

DAY three in San Francisco is a bit scarier than day one. For starters, I throw up my breakfast. *Shit.* Time to take a stroll to the nearest drugstore. As promiscuous as I am, I have never had a pregnancy scare. I take care of my shit. Always. So I find myself in unusual territory as I gaze at the nine million types of pregnancy tests. I find one and make my way to the register.

This really can't be happening to me.

I can't be pregnant.

I slept with so many men during my time at The Chamber. How will I begin to know who the father is? When the only person I would want to be the father is August. But like I shed Emmanuella to become Sapphire, he shed August to become Mason, and Mason doesn't do babies.

Mason runs The Chamber.

He is sex and control.

He is power.

He is money.

He isn't spit-up and diapers. Shit, neither am I.

When I get back to my room, I don't waste any time. I pee on the stick per the directions and I await the allotted amount of time. When the pink plus sign pops up, I think my heart actually stops.

"How am I pregnant? I'm pregnant! Me?"

I may as well forget about looking for Mason. If he didn't want me before, he certainly won't want me now.

21

*T*he documents I requested are at the front desk. *Perfect.* I ask the clerk for a sheet of hotel stationery and a pen. I grab a seat in the lounge and review the documents. Fifteen million dollars has been set up. The bulk of it is in a savings account and a smaller portion of it is in a checking account in Raimy Foster's name. I requested a bank card and checks so she will have immediate access to her funds.

I write her a brief note on the hotel stationery.

Ivory,

I am setting you free. I know that deep down you have always wanted to set out on your own. Perhaps you'll start your own Chamber. You are not meant to be a kept woman. You are built to be in a power position. It's who you are. I want that for you. Enclosed is your bank account information. The hotel is paid up for two months. Please stay. Enjoy Paris on me. Stay in the hotel as long as you like. Best of luck to you. You are strong and brave, and I know you will do well in anything you desire.

Mason

"How may I help you, Monsieur Wilde?" the clerk at the front desk asks me when I walk back to the counter.

"Yes. I would like this envelope delivered to my suite. My companion, Miss Ivory Deluere, must sign for this. I would like to have receipt of this delivered to me at the patisserie across the street."

"Understood, Monsieur Wilde. I will see to it myself."

"I will see to it that you are rewarded handsomely."

～

"A CAFÉ LATTE," I say when the stunning Parisian waitress takes my order. It is taking the clerk a rather long time. I am sure Ivory suspected the contents of the envelope the second it was delivered, and is demanding answers from the poor young man. I guess I could have warned him that she can be a handful.

It really isn't like she has a choice in the matter. A decision has been made, and if she knows me at all, it will only be another few moments before she tempers herself and realizes that it is over. I sip my latte and wait for the young man to arrive with my confirmation. Only a few more moments pass before he is crossing the narrow street toward me.

"Monsieur." He nods and hands me the receipt. "It is done. She is really quite a tough one," he says.

"Yes, I suppose a warning would have been appropriate."

"Next time, monsieur."

I hand the clerk five hundred euros. "Thank you very much for your assistance and your discretion."

He smiles in surprise at the size of the tip. "Monsieur, what of your things?" he asks.

"They're just things," I say, giving him a polite smile. I turn my attention to my latte, and the young clerk takes the cue and leaves. With the life I have appropriated for myself, I have never felt comfortable enough to let all of my walls down.

In the last ten years, I have never had problems with the authorities. No man who participates in The Chamber wants it to become public knowledge, so I never worry about the lottery winners. I treat my employees with respect, kindness, and lofty payment. I'm not naïve enough to blindly trust my employees, so I maintain special files on everyone. That is another reason I will miss working with Tyson—he was beyond loyal and the closest thing to a friend I have ever had, besides Sapphire. The girls fear me and the consequences to their families if they ever said a word. Nevertheless, over the years I have developed many fail-safes. One of them is to always place all of my vital belongings in a safe deposit box in a bank. Everything else will always be just *things*.

When I finish up my latte, I know what I must do.

22

MASON, NEW JERSEY

*W*hen the plane touches down at Newark Liberty International in New Jersey, I instantly feel excited, kind of like when I was about to have my first kiss. Maybe it is a mistake giving a twenty-two year old this much power over me. Who the fuck am I turning into, Mr. Sensitivity? Damn you, Emmanuella.

Truthfully, I shouldn't even be complaining about the control she has over me because I am enjoying all of the new feelings I am experiencing. The waiting driver takes me directly to East Brunswick. I grow more and more enthused the closer we get to her house. By the time we pull up to Emmanuella's, my excitement takes an unexpected turn. I'm nervous. Yet another emotion I am unaccustomed to. I can't remember the last time I felt so unsure of myself. What if she doesn't want to come with me? What then?

"Just wait here. We will be right back," I tell the driver, hoping my positive words will help ensure that she will come back with me.

I step out of the sedan and make my way up the drive. In mere moments she will be in my arms again, and I will never let her go. I am in awe of her. She changed me without asking me to change, without knowing the power she has to make me see possibilities. I became someone I never imagined I could be in her arms and under her gaze. I became less monster and more man each day.

I ring the doorbell.

A young woman who looks almost identical to Emmanuella opens the door. I immediately recognize her as Gabriella, Emmanuella's younger sister. She is beautiful. If I were even more of a monster, I might even consider adding her to a future Chamber. But I can't even say how sure I am of The Chamber's future anymore. What if Emmanuella and I move to Brisbane for a year, just the two of us?

"Hi. Can I help you?" she asks.

"You must be Gabriella. I have heard a lot about you. I am a friend of your sister, Emmanuella's. My name is Mason. Is she here?"

She steps outside, closing the door behind her. She doesn't invite me in. I guess she figures any friend of Emmanuella's wouldn't be welcome inside.

"She left. She hopped on a plane. My parents kind of made it impossible for her to stay here, what with the cleansings and exorcisms," she says, rolling her eyes.

"What?"

She shakes her head and waves her hand across her face dismissing what she just said. But I can't. I am more than a monster for sending the woman I love back to such an awful family. They believe she is evil? Don't they know that old quote about people who live in glass houses? I have a sudden urge to ask for water. So I can be invited inside and meet Emmanuella's *wonderful* parents myself.

"You're him, aren't you? The one she fell in love with? You know, she really wanted to stay with you. Why did you send her away?"

"Because I'm an idiot. I didn't know that I loved her until she was gone. So, she told you about me?" I have an overwhelming urge to smile, so I do. It's one of those stupid smiles that I can't wipe off my face.

"Not much. Just that she didn't want to leave you. That's all."

"Well, I was a fool to let her go. Do you know where she went?"

She nods.

"So, are you gonna tell me where she is?"

She holds up a finger to me. I have no choice but to wait. Then she pulls out her cell phone, pushes a couple of buttons, then puts the phone to her face. She walks a couple of steps from me, but I follow. She turns and looks at me with venom in her eyes, before stepping further away. This time, I don't follow. They run hot in this family. If I want her help, I'd better keep my ass in this spot. Now I have to strain to hear.

"Hi, sis."

I wish I could hear what Emmanuella is saying on the other end.

"I'm checking in," Gabriella says. "How's your new city treating you?"

She purposely didn't mention her location.

"What!" Oh my goodness, are you okay? Do you need me to come to you?"

What? What does she mean? I am at her side at once. I am about to snatch the phone away, but I think better of it and remain calm.

"Can I ask you a question? Do you still wish you stayed there?"

I am not privy to her answer to this question, either. I am going to explode with impatience.

"Sis, you can't know that. You haven't even given him the chance to make that decision. How can you say it's too late? What if he really loves you?" She glances up at me.

I endure another stretch of silence.

"Listen, if you need me to be on a plane, I will. Just let me know. I have to go now. *Mãe* is calling me," she lies. "I love you, too." She hangs up and looks at me then back at her front door. "You wanna take a walk?" she asks me.

"Um, okay."

We start out down the drive. I motion to the driver to give us a minute. We continue onto the sidewalk and down the street a few feet before she turns to me.

"She is in San Francisco," she says.

"Is she okay?" I reach out and grab her arm. I don't squeeze it. I am holding on to her so I don't panic.

"Sort of."

"What does 'sort of' mean?"

"Let's just say, you probably won't want to go running to find her now." She looks up at me with deadpan expression.

What the fuck is going on? What could possibly be so bad that I wouldn't want to find her? "Can you tell me what's going on so I can make that decision myself, please?"

"Okay." She takes a couple of steps farther down the street. I follow, right on her heels. She is making me crazy. "I'm going to be an aunt."

I stop dead in my tracks. "She's pregnant?" *Fuck.*

"Yep. And she's in San Francisco, freaking the hell out. She never wanted to have kids. Now she's pregnant and all alone." She turns and starts walking away, back toward the house. "She is staying at the Ritz-Carlton in San Francisco under the name Sapphire Emmanuel if you decide you want to go after her." She continues walking away.

"Thank you," I call after her before she disappears into the house.

Shit. A baby. What the hell do I know about being a fucking father? And whose baby is it? Fuck. This changes everything.

I slide my defeated body into the sedan. "The airport, please."

I have no idea where I am going. I can't go back to Paris, not that I want to. That is not my style, anyway. Ivory and I were done the second I decided I wanted more from life. But I am not sure I want *that* much more. Diapers and poop, spit-up and crying.

How can I be both a parent and The Chamber's master?

August *and* Mason?

I don't know where I am going right now. This is where having someone to talk to about my problems, friends or a family, would be beneficial. Before now, I never really had any problems. It is amazing how life can change on a dime. Suddenly, I know exactly where I am going.

~

I GET off the plane in Aspen, Colorado, my birthplace. I've always said I'd never go back, but I am at the biggest crossroads of my entire life. How can I be fit to be a parent when the only examples I have are my parents?

I haven't been home since I was seventeen. I know my parents are both well because I check in on them every once in a while. I'm thirty now, a grown man.

After a thirty-minute car ride the driver pulls up to the guarded gate of my family's estate.

"I'm August Mitchell, here to see my parents," I say to the guard.

The guard calls up to the house and within seconds the gates are sliding open. The tree-lined drive is at least a quarter mile from the estate. It really is beautiful—the kind of place to raise a family. Aspen has all four seasons, and Mitchell Manor has everything a kid could desire. Emmanuella and I would be happy raising a family here. *If* I were to give it all up.

It is all mine, after all.

My parents put it on the market six years ago when they were ready to retire and travel. This place requires a great deal of upkeep. So I bought it from them, with instructions from my attorney to request that they would still live here at least part of the year. I could've asked them to give me the estate instead of selling it, but for some stubborn reason, I couldn't imagine letting them give me anything. I am a man. I can take care of myself. If I want something, I acquire it.

When we arrive at the entrance, my mother and father are waiting for me. They look the same, just older. My father, who I get my height from, is still tall and athletic. I'm sure he is far too vain to gain a pound. My mother, who I get my looks from, is still a raven-haired beauty. It has been thirteen years since we have laid eyes on each other. When I climb out of the car, I steady myself for our unemotional reunion.

"August!" My mother runs up to me and wraps me in a tight embrace. My father joins her, hugging us both.

What the hell is this? I can count on one hand the times my parents have hugged me. "Okay, hi." I turn to the driver and motion for him to stay. I don't know how long this visit is going to take. I walk into the house with them, arm in arm.

They are freaking me the fuck out.

The entry is just as vast and opulent as I remember, with high, vaulted ceilings, pine pillars separating the living spaces, and eclectic art hanging on the walls. The entire back wall of the house is floor to ceiling windows that overlook a majestic view that I enjoyed staring at as a child.

"Please, son, have a seat."

I do as they ask.

"What a wonderful surprise, August. How have you been?" Mom gushes.

"Fine, Mother. And you and Father?"

A middle-aged maid comes into the room. She is dressed impeccably in black and white without a hair out of place. "Madame, would you like coffee or tea for your guest?" She stands waiting for my mother to answer.

"He is no guest, Maggie. He is the reluctant heir to our empire, and the owner of this estate," my father says. "This is our son, August."

"My apologies, Mr. August, sir. Would you like coffee or tea?"

"Coffee will do fine, Maggie, and August is fine." Mason would be finer, but that is not who I am right now. In light of the choice I have to make, I don't know if I will ever be Mason again.

She walks away, leaving me and my parents in awkward silence. I clear my dry throat. "So, you guys look good," I say.

"So do you, August," my father says. "I'm just going to cut to the chase, son. Where have you been? We haven't heard a word from you in thirteen years, except for the sale of the estate."

I straighten in my seat. My parents wait for me to answer. Maggie breaks the silence, returning with our coffee in Grandma Mitchell's china.

"Well, you see," I pause to take a long swig of my coffee. It's piping hot, just like I like it, and it's black, just like my cold heart. I scoot to the edge of my seat. "Growing up, you and Mom felt that acquiring the family fortune was more important than raising your child. Trust me, I have no hard feelings about that. It made me stronger. So, I decided to test the theory. I set out to acquire my own fortune."

"And?" my father asks.

"As it turns out, the apple doesn't fall far from the tree. You would find my financial portfolio very impressive."

"What do you do?" my mother asks, taking a sip of her coffee.

I sit back in my chair and relax. I have nothing to prove. I am only the forgotten son. My parents are the ones who have to answer for their mistakes where I am concerned. I continue drinking my coffee. The blend is pleasing to my palate and the aroma is sensational. I must ask Maggie what blend this is. "Let's just say that I am in acquisitions and mergers." That's all I offer them.

"Are you married? Any children?" my mother asks.

I choke on my coffee at the mention of children, my resolve temporarily shaken.

"Not at the moment." *But that could all change very soon.*

I get up and take in the house. To my surprise, there are pictures of me everywhere. To anyone visiting, it looks like my parents are very proud of me. Granted, the pictures stop at a teenaged me. Very few pictures show us together. I take the winding staircase two steps at a time.

When I open the door to my room it is just how I left it. *Sports Illustrated* and Victoria's Secret models pictures cover the walls. My kickboxing gear is in the corner, with my heavy bag still hanging from the ceiling. I got so strong by the time I was fourteen, my dad had to hire a professional to add secondary beams into the ceiling so I didn't destroy the house. My four-poster bed and dresser set are still in place. Growing up, I don't know how many hours I spent sitting in my window seat, looking out at the breathtaking Aspen view. It's beautiful any time of the year.

I make my way downstairs. My parents haven't moved. "So, I'll bet you guys are wondering why I came back after all this time."

They both nod.

I am so much more Mason than I am August. I can't help it. I am more at ease and more myself under the guise of Mason Wilde than I ever was as August Mitchell. I can tell my presence is rattling them, because they are holding on to one another like I am an intruder instead of their son.

"Did you enjoy having me? I mean, I guess I should ask, why did you have me? Because I feel like I was mostly invisible to you both."

I sit down and face them, my hands resting casually on my lap. I am the monster and the monster wants answers. There is no way I can move forward with my life without having this very important conversation. I stare at them both, waiting.

After a long pause my mother speaks up first. "We never meant it to be that way. When you were born, it was the happiest day of our lives. We loved you so much. We still love you." My mother scoots forward. "Your dad's business had really started to take off. He didn't want to live in his father's shadow or take his money. He always wanted to make it on his own."

Sounds familiar.

"We were so hell-bent on making a name for ourselves and for you, August." She takes my hands in hers.

It takes everything in my power to allow this contact. The only other person in my life who I have let touch me in such a personal way is Emmanuella.

"We forgot to raise you. We regret it every day. Because we made this fortune for you, and just when the money was working for us, and we were able to give you the time and attention you deserved, you were gone." Tears flood my mother's face.

"Son, we are so sorry. We love you so much," my father adds.

Damn. I hadn't expected this. They seem genuinely sorry.

"Regret is a sharp-toothed bitch, son," my father says. Do you think you could ever forgive us? Can we start again?"

How can I say no? I know for a fact the monster would have. But I am not only the monster. I am also August, thanks to Emmanuella.

"I think we can try," I say. I will never admit how choked up I am.

My mother and father embrace me. For the first time in my life, I am part of a family again. What is happening to me? Is love that strong an emotion?

I stay and have lunch in my childhood home. I even sip a Jameson and Coke with my father. And just like that, I can see us visiting for the holidays and birthdays. I would love to bring Emmanuella here during ski season. I don't tell them, but I am even considering the possibility of raising my own family in this house.

The dining table looks out over the backyard. The estate sits on over twenty acres. There are horse stables and two Olympic-sized swimming pools, one indoor and one outdoor.

There's a playground with swings, slides, and a trampoline. It's perfect for a family. I'm freaking out because I am imagining one, no matter if the kid is mine or not. My dead heart started beating in the presence of Emmanuella, and I will give everything up to keep it beating. *Fuck.*

23

SAPPHIRE, SAN FRANCISCO

*M*y choices have dwindled before my eyes. *Pregnant.* What's worse than pregnant? Well, there's the fact that I spent the last year with a slew of men, and any one of them could be the father. When I leave my suite very early in the morning I wind up at, of all places, a fucking baby boutique. I have no explanation of how I got up here.

There is baby shit everywhere.

I almost heave up what little breakfast I have in my stomach, looking around at all of the baby clothes, diapers, strollers, and car seats. What in the world am I getting myself into? How am I even fit to be a mother? Parenthood should require some type of license. I mean, as tough of a job as it is, I can't believe that everyone is meant to, or should have children just because we are biologically capable. I know I don't have a fucking clue.

"May I help you find something, dear?" the salesperson asks me. She is also expecting. I don't know how far along she is, but she definitely has a baby bump.

"Just looking for a gift for a friend," I lie.

"For a boy or a girl?" the sales lady inquires.

"I don't know yet. I mean, my friend doesn't know. It's too early," I say.

The purse of her lips is a dead giveaway that she knows that I am full of shit, and very much knocked-up. "Take all the time you need. I will be over there if you have any questions." She gestures toward the register.

I give her the friendliest smile I can muster up under the circumstances and continue looking around.

I don't keep track of how much time I spend in the tiny boutique. Everything is so soft and delicate.

Like the life growing inside me.

This is wrong on so many levels. I look around just to torture myself. Instead of beautiful clothes and sexy nights with Mason, my life will be full of poopy diapers and baby spit-up. My dream of being with Mason is over before it even begins. There is no point trying to find him now. The master of the secretive Chamber isn't going to want to share the throne with a knocked-up ex-Chambermaid. I can see how well that idea would fit into his life plan.

I can't resist the urge to buy a soft plush monkey with big purple eyes. It's my baby's first gift. I think I will call him Murple. He is much too big to fit into a crib. *Oh my goodness, a crib.*

On my way back to the hotel, Murple and I stop off at a local deli so I can grab a simple lunch of soup and salad. The accessibility of San Francisco is already growing on me. Everything is within walking distance from my hotel.

What I eat doesn't matter much to me right now. Nothing sounds good these days, and I can't keep anything down. Hopefully, my lunch and my tummy will play nice.

Back at the hotel, I make my way toward the elevator. I wonder if I should call my sister back and take her up on her offer to stay with me. At least if Gabriella is here I won't have to endure this alone. I hate being alone for too long. Even this suite is getting too lonesome and quiet for me. It's only when

I walk into the room and set my room key, lunch, and purse on the dining room table that I touch my stomach and realize I will never be alone again. "What am I going to do with you? I guess it's just you and me, kid."

"Don't I get a say in the matter?"

I look up to see Mason sitting in the living room of my suite with flowers and a giant stuffed bear in his hands.

My face must be sheet-white because I swear all of my blood pools into my feet and my heart drops to my stomach. "Mason?"

"I believe that would be August to you." He stands and crosses the room quickly toward me. "I have missed you so." He wraps me into a loving embrace, and I can't help the tears of joy that fall from my eyes. "What have you done to me, you crazy woman?"

"How did you find me?" I ask. I gaze into his beautiful face.

He takes both hands and gently brushes my tears away with his thumbs. He leads me to the sofa. "Your sister, Gabriella. She also told me that you are expecting," he says.

"Yes. I'm sorry."

"For what exactly?"

"Getting pregnant."

"Dear, don't be sorry. We took all necessary precautions, right?"

"Yes," I say through sniffles. I want to know why he came, but I fear his answer. What if he isn't here to take me back? He wraps his arms around me, and I let a waterfall flow. I cry tears of relief that he is here, tears of fear of being a mother, and tears of worry that he might leave me again.

"Are you okay?"

"I am now that you are here."

"I'm so sorry it took me this long," he says, rubbing his hand down my thigh. I feel warm and safe.

I shrug my shoulders, taking in and releasing a deep breath. "Why are you here?" I ask him. I can't take any action

for granted. I don't have the strength to assume anymore. I
mean, based on my assumptions I thought I was never
getting sent home, and I was wrong. *All cards on the table,
buddy.*

"Emmanuella, what do you mean? I came back for you. I
was in Paris, and I flew to New Jersey, and then here."

He turns my face to his. But I can't look at him. How can
anyone want me like this?

"Will you look at me?"

I don't want to, but Mason has a power over me. He oozes
sex from every pore. Those eyes have a way of traveling
depths until they reach my soul. I do as I am told, even
though at this moment I am so afraid of him. I have given
him so much power over my heart, and he can break it into a
million pieces if he wants. Not that he would. I know him,
and he is much kinder than anyone knows.

"I am willing to give it all up and be August and
Emmanuella for you, for us, and for the baby you are carrying. For you, I want to shed the monster and be the man."

Is he serious? For me? This must be some sort of dream. I
don't understand how a girl like me, barely a woman,
possesses what is necessary to tame a beast. I mean, this is the
fantasy, the dream I have wanted from the day I met him. But
isn't that the way of dreams? Often enough, we dream them,
sometimes the same dream over and over, but deep down
inside we know that most will never really manifest. Unless I
am proof that dreaming is not a pastime, and if there is desire
behind the dream, it can and will come true. Mason being
here against all odds must be proof of that. Not only does he
want me, he wants to change because of me. But is that what I
want? Is that who I fell in love with? Would I love him the
same if I met him as August Mitchell, businessman? Probably
not, because I am every bit the monster he is.

"But what if I want the monster and the man?" I stare
deep into his eyes. My deep browns peer into his dazzling

blues. I don't bother blinking. I want him to see what I want, what I feel for him.

"You want the monster?" he asks. I see hope in his eyes.

I nod. "Your monster and mine belong together," I tell him.

"I love you," he says.

Now I am crying harder because of pure joy. Not only does he want me, but he loves me. "What about the baby?"

"I guess we are about to become fucking parents, as fucked up as that sounds." Neither of us can help bursting out laughing at the idea. "I know, it has to be the craziest thing I have ever heard, but our child will want for nothing," he says.

I wrap my arms around him and squeeze him in a loving embrace. He obviously doesn't care if the baby is his or not, but I still need to be sure. "Are you going to want a paternity test?" I ask. I fear the answer, but the last thing I need is a gut punch down the road.

"Hell, no. You honestly think with all the birth control I had you on that any of those bastards' sperm could penetrate through but mine?"

I kiss him hard on the lips. "You are a cocky son of a bitch, and I love you even more for it."

"I know. Why do you think I'm here? There is no one else on this planet who can love me with all the fucked-up shit I have going on. Then to actually fall in love back? Well, damn. If that ain't a match made in heaven, I don't know what is."

"Come on, Mason. Do you really think you and I are going to heaven?"

"Not for one minute."

Then our lips are on one another's. I need him buried inside me now to be one hundred percent sure.

What happens next is what I dream about every night. Mason picks me up and throws me over his shoulder. He smacks my behind and squeezes after each swift smack.

"Where are you taking me?" I say in between squeals and giggles.

"Bedroom."

"Why?"

"Today, I am the fucking monster. I have plenty of time to show you the man."

He tosses me onto the bed as we tear wildly at each other's clothes. I almost come on the spot.

Mason stands before me with only his pants on, hanging low on his hips in a way that blows my fucking mind. I can see a part of the V that goes underneath his waistline. I can also see a hint of his happy trail. His body is a-fucking-mazing. His toned and muscled chest and washboard abs along with his bad-boy looks... Whoa, he has a half sleeve on his right arm. *Where did that come from?* Mason hid every feature that would make him identifiable in The Chamber. I never even knew he had tattoos. *Hell, yes! He is all mine?*

When his cock springs free, I think I am on it before he can step out of his pants. I go tow work sucking Mason's cock as if it is made of gold—something that deserves a place of honor. My tongue plays with the tip in slow, delicious circles. His moaning only drives me forward. I sink my entire mouth around the shaft, up and down, up and down, sucking when I get to the tip. Over and over I worship his cock, my cock.

"I don't want to come like this. I want to come inside you, Emmanuella," he says in between gasps as he gently pushes me off him and pulls his cock out of my mouth.

He lies back onto the bed and I follow without skipping a beat. I take his precious cock into my hand, rubbing my hand up and down his pristine shaft.

"Mmmm," he moans.

Through hooded eyes I gaze at him before I sink down onto him. My walls fill in every possible space. I almost come on the spot. My eyes roll as I start a slow, rhythmic grind on his cock. Mason's busy hands touch and caress every part of me—my breasts, my ass, my waist. He pulls me down onto him as I grind harder. We both come apart at the same time, convulsing and shuddering.

"You are mine, Emmanuella, and I fucking love you. I have never said I love you to a single person in my life," he says. Then he kisses me.

His lips take mine hostage as his tongue plays wicked games with mine. I almost come again as I feel his cock regaining its strength inside me. It never takes my favorite cock long to be ready for another round.

Mason flips me over, and now I am on my back. He raises up onto his knees without us ever separating. He doesn't move, he just watches me. Studies me. "Will you fucking be my wife?"

"I might be the monster," he continues, "but I think I am legally allowed to marry anyone I chose." Then he slams his cock deep inside of me.

"What about Ivory?" I pant heavily.

"Who?" he asks, slamming his cock into me again.

Oh my fuck, this feels amazing.

"Well, then in that case, not just yes, but hell fucking yes I will be your wife!" I yell.

The monster comes alive at once. Mason is relentless in his thrusts and I take them all with joy, until we are both coming again. If there is a heaven on earth, this must be it. My heart is home.

We pass out entangled in each other's arms.

24

SAPPHIRE, SAN FRANCISCO

"What should we do today?" I ask, rolling over onto Mason's muscular chest. He smells like the piney outdoors, sweet musk, and sex.

"Before or after we shower?"

"After."

He kisses me quickly on the lips and hops out of bed. Naked, Mason is fucking hot. He's tall and lean with the muscles of a serious athlete. I want to bite his ass as he walks away. I wait for him to return. I can't believe I am getting exactly what I want. He wants me and the baby. He wants me to be his wife. Well, yesterday he did. Today he may think he has lost his fucking mind. I want him so much my heart is swollen with love. He wants to be the man for me. Did I accidentally rub up against a magic lamp?

"How did you find me?" I yell above the sound of rushing water. I probably shouldn't ask the evil mastermind that question. He could find a needle in a haystack.

"I was there with your sister when she called you," he yells back.

"What?" Now I am the one crossing the room in the buff.

"You met my sister?"

"Yep." He runs his hand under the tap to test the water temperature. "Your parent's home was the first place I went to. I told her not to tell you I was there so I could surprise you. Were you surprised?"

"Best surprise of my life, so far." My sneaky little sister. I will have to thank her later. "I thought we were taking a shower?" I ask when I see the water and bubbles rising in the tub.

He turns to me, his eyes full of excitement and wonder. It feels amazing knowing that I put that smile on his face and that look in his eyes. "Isn't this what the man would do?"

He makes me swoon. I flutter my eyelashes at him. "I think I am starting to love the man almost as much as I love the monster."

"We'll see about that." He winks.

When the tub is sufficiently full, we both ease in. The water is hot, but tolerable. A bubble bath with the man? Who knew?

Mason takes a seat in the tub and I sit in front of him, his full erection pressing against my back. I lean my head back against his chest while his arms wrap around me.

In another unexpected gesture of hearts and flowers, Mason picks up my bath sponge, adds some lavender body wash to it, and begins to wash me. I close my eyes as he runs the sponge over my shoulders and neck. A girl could get used to this. I sit forward so that he can reach my back. "Mmm."

When I am thoroughly washed, I turn around so that I can wash him. He too closes his eyes as I cherish his chiseled chest and abs, only I don't use the sponge. I load body wash into my hands.

"Mmm," he says.

And I feel it. The feeling is overwhelming. How the two of us found each other can only be explained as fated. Two love-starved people who didn't come from abusive or broken homes, but didn't receive the love or attention we deserved. *I wonder if that is why we are both sex addicts? Are we filling a void?* Now we've been brought together, and I can see in Mason's relaxed body and deep moans that he wants to be loved and cherished. Neither of us would ever admit what we lack or crave. Who would? To admit what you are missing is to accept the loss and mourn it. To deny its existence is a way to power on and rise above it. That is what Mason and I have always done—stayed strong in the wake of where our parents fell short.

He isn't just Mason, nor am I just Sapphire. We are and will always be August and Emmanuella. Because in truth, all we ever wanted our entire lives was to be accepted for who we are and be loved anyway.

His eyes open slowly, and I am caught staring at him.

The smile that crosses his face is delicious and loving. "Now that you have said yes to marrying me, we have to do three things."

I smile in return and stop bathing him. "Oh, yeah?" I turn around, my back resting against his chest. His arms are around me at once. "My curiosity is piqued."

"Ring shopping. My folks' house. And then yours."

"What?" I turn around and face him in the tub, sending a wave of water onto the bathroom floor.

"Well, in my search for you I realized if I'm going to be a father to our baby, I'd need to talk to my parents. They are the only family I have. We've reconciled, and I can't wait for them to meet you."

I throw my arms around him, splashing more water onto the floor. "I am so happy for you, Mason."

He hugs me in return, and I believe I hear a soft almost giggle-laugh escape him. He is happy.

"I hardly see there being any reason that we need to drag my folks into this, though," I say.

"Well, I do, and I am the man in this relationship."

"Oh, so bossy. I hope you aren't always the man. I crave the monster as much as the man, you know," I remind him.

"I know. Come on, you dirty girl. We need to get out of this water and go to Tiffany's so I can get you a proper engagement ring."

I jump up and he smacks my wet ass when I stand. The room spins and the nausea returns.

"Are you okay?" he asks, grabbing a towel and wrapping it around me.

"Yeah. Just this baby working its magic on me. Everything smells stronger, and I get dizzy and sick to my stomach."

He pulls me close to him. "I got you, baby."

The words soothe my soul.

WE QUICKLY DRY off and dress, then hop into a waiting sedan.

I speak in code because of the driver. "So in light of *all* that is happening, what is to become of our special place? I don't want you to give it up. It is such a big part of you, and it is where we met and fell in love."

"Really? I mean, I hadn't really thought of what to do about it, to be honest. But in light of our present circumstances, I hardly see how it could work," he says, rubbing my stomach.

"Oh, I am sure we could work all of this out. Knowing you, there will be plenty of space for a special *family* wing," I whisper the word family. "Not that I will miss her, but what happened to Ivory? I need to know." I really don't want to see her face again. "Did she leave? Or will I be making her acquaintance again soon?"

"She's gone," he says.

I am unable to hide my surprise, and frankly my happiness. She hated me. "Really? She left?"

"No. She made me choose," he says, now stroking my hand softly.

"Choose what?"

"Between her and you."

He surprises me at every turn. "You, sir, are amazing." I squeeze his hand.

When we pull up in front of Tiffany & Co., I am squirming with excitement. It is amazing how the things I never thought I wanted in my entire life are now all I can think of. I have a life filled with possibilities, romance, and a real family. He has changed me.

Mason stops outside the jewelry store. "Are you sure about this?" he asks.

"You and me at the helm of the mighty Chamber? Husband and wife? I think it could work. What about you?" I ask.

"I know it can work. Except this time, you are mine. I don't want you fucking anybody but me."

"Deal. What about you?"

"I don't want me fucking anybody but you either," he says.

"I love you so much, Mason."

"Enough of the Mason. I am only Mason there. With you I am and will always be August, and you are my Emmanuella —the one who cast a spell on me." He grasps my chin and kisses me. "I love you, too."

～

I HAVE NEVER SEEN anything as beautiful as my engagement ring. The white gold band is channel-set with round brilliant diamonds that complement the two-carat classic round Tiffany-cut diamond. The white light is blinding. I can't stop staring at it. I also can't stop the face-splitting smile. He even got down on one knee inside the jewelry store before he slid it onto my finger.

We even got matching channel-set diamond bands for the big day.

"Are you happy?"

"Happier than I ever thought I could be," I tell him.

When we walk out, there is the most exquisite sports car parked right in front of the store. It's sex on wheels—a sleek, deep maroon vehicle with black accents. Lethal. *Hmph, rich people. If anyone else had the audacity to park their car there, it would be towed for sure. Wait, I am a rich person, too.* I don't know if I will ever get used to that idea. I certainly don't think like a rich person.

"What are you doing?" I ask when August opens the passenger-side door, gesturing for me to get in.

"I bought this baby while you were dressing this morning. I had it delivered here. No more whispered conversations in the back seat of a sedan."

I slide inside. The leather is so soft, I actually melt into it. I watch the love of my life walk around our new, beautiful car. He doesn't walk. He glides. "What kind of car is this?" I ask when he slides behind the wheel.

"It's called a Pagani Huayra." He starts the car. It purrs to life.

"Must be nice to have everything you want at your finger-tips," I say.

The smile on his face is alarming. I still can't believe that he is all mine. What did I do to get so lucky?

"It will take you some getting used to, but you soon will. Truth be told, this is all because of you. I am usually more methodical. I wouldn't consider myself a spur-of-the-moment kind of guy."

"Me?"

"Yes. Seems like you are turning me into some sort of upright citizen who checks in on his family. Now I'm a 'hearts and flowers' guy who proposes marriage. Before you, I was the Chamber Master, and now for you, I am willing to give it all up."

I can't help the smile that is now taking up half of my face. He says that I am changing him, but, really, he is changing me. I was never one for hearts, romance, flowers, and candy.

Fuck me and let me go home was more my M.O.

Now I'm constantly professing my love to Mason. I mean, August. I'm pledging monogamy. And he says I bewitched him. I think he also possesses some mojo. Or, maybe it's that we've both met our equals. I need him like I need air, water, and heat. He makes me see life through different eyes. With him, I can dream of a family of my own...a home. Only a freak like him can tame a freak like me.

"Where to now?" I ask.

"I was thinking we could take the 101 to the coastal scenic route down to L.A. Then we'll head to Vegas and get hitched. I've always wanted to do that. Not the getting married part, but the drive down the coast."

"Really?" I am bouncing with excitement in my seat.

"Yes, and don't get mad at me, okay..." he starts.

My face falls. "Why would I ever get mad at you?"

"Oh, I have seen your hot side." He fishes an envelope from his jacket and hands it to me. "Remember, don't be mad."

I pull the contents from the envelope and begin to inspect them. "I don't understand." I stare at his profile.

"I changed your name back to Emmanuella, legally."

"Why?" I am not mad, really, I just don't understand.

"Because I fell in love with Emmanuella, not Sapphire. Emmanuella turned me into August. I don't want to marry Sapphire, I want to marry you. Is that okay?"

I inhale. It's all here—everything changed back to my old name. "Okay."

"Okay? Just okay?" He takes his eyes off the road and stares at me like I have six heads.

"You expected me to put up more of a fight?" I tease.

"Frankly, yes."

"Nope. I'm getting everything that I want, and some things I didn't even know I wanted. If keeping my name makes you happy, then it is the least I can do," I say.

"I fucking love you, girl!" he yells in an expression of joy.

"I know."

25

SAPPHIRE, LAS VEGAS

"So, do billionaires ever have to do anything for themselves?" I ask when our marriage license is delivered to our Bellagio suite.

"Name one person alive who would stand in a long line if there was a way around it," he says.

"True. I could have used one of those line people at Disneyland."

"Noted." Mason reaches for the license and leads me to the couch. "I need to talk to you before we make this official."

"Okay." I sit and wait for this apparently important conversation.

Mason takes a seat next to me. *He is serious.* "Do you really think I deserve this much happiness? I mean, I am the monster. For the past ten years I have taken women from their homes and made sex slaves out of them. How is it that I deserve the happy ending? The amazing wife, the white picket fence, the beautiful family..." he confesses.

Oh, my poor dear Mason. The guilt he feels is so unexpected.

I scoot in closer to him, and I look deep into his eyes.

"Okay, I can see how you would feel that way about yourself, but the same can be said about me. I have been giving myself up to random guys since ninth grade. I was branded the school slut. Sure, I wore the badge with honor. I had no other choice but to accept it. That doesn't mean either of us deserves to be unhappy and alone forever."

His rolling eyes tell me he ain't buyin' what I'm sellin'.

"Sure, you ran or run The Chamber, but even in that you showed that you are a good person. Everyone you employ is well taken care of. Every girl who you take is treated like a princess. They're showered with a lavish lifestyle for one year and then you make them millionaires and deliver them back to their front doorsteps. You are hardly a cruel man. Well, maybe you're a little fucked up and twisted, but who isn't?"

To this, he snorts. "Would you still want to do this whole thing if I told you after this last Chamber I don't want to do it anymore? I just want to be with you. Raise our baby in Aspen. Live a real life. We could do whatever we want."

He is serious. I don't think he knows what I will say. Does he believe I only want him for The Chamber? Does he not know how much I love him? "Let' make this the Final Chamber. We'll make a go of it in Brisbane, and have the time of our lives. Then we'll retire. I only want you, Mr. August Mitchell, and I will take you any way that I can get you. Even if that means a little less monster and a little more man."

With that he is on me. He lets me know with each kiss and caress how happy I have made him.

"By the way, baby, you never have to worry about our little monster. Did I mention that my house, I mean our house, in Aspen has a three-thousand-square-foot basement area that would make the perfect play area?"

"Well, I am intrigued! And now that you know that I want you for you, and not your chosen career path, can we get to the part where I become your fucking wife?"

Mason stands, pulling me up with him. "Hell, yes."

Mason takes my hand and we head down to the Bellagio

Chapel. We look the part of bride and groom. Mason is wearing a gorgeous black Michael Kors suit, and I am wearing a white—yes, white—Vera Wang gown. I am nervous when we reach the chapel doors until I look up at Mason standing on my right.

He takes my hand and places it over his heart. "You feel that?"

"Your heartbeat?"

"It was cold and dead, and it didn't start beating until you came into my life."

Happiness takes over my face. He is the man I love, and we are taking this journey together. This is what I want. He is what I want. Any doubt or fear that I had was dispelled in an instant. I squeeze his hand and he returns the gesture. We walk into the chapel and we don't look back.

EPILOGUE

*M*y life turned out more different than I could have ever imagined. We decided that we would forever be Sapphire and Emmanuella, Mason and August, depending on the moment and time. We decided that it doesn't matter who the father of the baby is. We will never do a test, because it just doesn't fucking matter.

We visit Mason's family in Aspen. They really are lovely people. They may not have done a good job being nurturing parents to him growing up, but I can tell they are more than willing and ready to make up for all of the lost time. They are thrilled about the baby and the news of our marriage. Mason's mother told me to call her "Mom" and even took me on a tour of the house, showing me possible options for the baby's room. When Mason told them that we would soon come back to Aspen for good they were ecstatic. His dad is having the three-thousand-square-foot guesthouse prepared so they can downsize, and we will have the big house to ourselves. With over ten thousand square feet of living space, I told them they didn't really have to move out, but they insisted.

We decide to hold off on visiting my parents for a while. The timing of the baby might raise some eyebrows, seeing how I was missing for an entire year. Truth be told, I am in no rush.

Brisbane, Australia is the perfect spot for this year's Chamber. The hidden location is palatial, and virtually untraceable. The rest of the staff began arriving—to my surprise, hooded just as I had been over a year ago. I didn't have to ask my husband the reason for the security. Very few members of his team are actually privy to the actual location. Our wing is completely separate from the rest of The Chamber. Mason went out of his way to make it a comfortable home.

I plan to be included in every phase of this year's Chamber, especially since it will be our last, beginning with the arrival of the new Chambermaids and their naming, with one catch. We're going legit. Seven women were hired for one year, not taken. Mason actually loved the idea, not only is it guilt-free, but he only spends seven million on salaries, a far cry from the twenty-eight he usually spends.

In August, I make a special solo trip to California to take my place by my Chamber sister's side as she marries her love. My red gown has to be altered to make room for my growing belly. I decide it is in our best interest, and that of the baby that I am carrying, that I don't report to any of my sisters that I found my love. As far as they know, I am raising my baby alone. It is better that way. Most will not approve of my desire to be a part of The Chamber's continued existence, no matter how many changes we've made to improve upon it. They don't understand, and I will never judge them for that.

I enjoyed spending time with my sisters. Everyone looks happy and adjusted with their lives. Gabriella joins me in Malibu and we make a mini vacation of the trip. We even check out Disneyland. I can't ride most of the rides in my present condition, but the energy is palpable.

I explain to my sister that I will be in less contact for a while. I don't tell her that I have been in Australia, only that Mason and I are going off-grid for a while. I can also never refer to him as August to anyone, ever. We'll have this one last hoorah before we settle down in Aspen to raise our family.

My sister doesn't know it, but I have plans to bring her to Aspen.

When I return to Australia a week later, Mason has completely remodeled our suite to include a nursery.

What he doesn't realize, and I soon hope to make him understand, is that no matter what my documents say, I am Sapphire, and he is Mason. And together, at least for this final year, we are The Chamber.

Read Poisoned Ivy, the next book in the Seven Chambers series.

POISONED IVY SAMPLE

Chapter One
Maeve Counting the Days

It has been nine months since I was nabbed from the athletic club and brought to The Chamber. That is: two hundred and seventy days; six thousand four hundred and eighty hours; three hundred eighty-eight thousand, eight hundred minutes; and twenty-three million, three hundred and twenty-eight thousand seconds. Yes, I am counting, because each and every passing, precious second, minute, hour, and day means that even though I have lost a little more of myself, I am closer to going home. Closer to shedding the name Ivy and all of the horror that comes with it. That is, if Mason stays true to his word our first night here, and we are actually released. I'm not sure that there will be enough of me to make it home. But whatever is left, I will drag it home and my love will help me become whole again.

You see, I am not as strong as the other girls. I have always had what my mother called "a fragile constitution" growing up, probably because I am not a stranger to traumatic events.

Mason has amassed quite the spread. Most of the girls here are strong, and will most likely leave this tragic experience even stronger, with battle wounds that they will wear as badges. I believe that those are the type of girls that the sadistic Mason Wilde should shoot for, because his aim was off on a few of us.

Me, Violet, and Sunshine are the weakest links in the chain, and we may not survive.

Raven is my roommate and I have seen her in action. She is calculating, always watching, always studying. She hasn't shed one visible tear since the day we got here. She may look like a beauty queen, but she is tough as nails. Sapphire, I swear, is enjoying herself here. I wouldn't be surprised if she asked to stay on and work here at the end of our year.

If there is an end.

Sky, who I believe belongs in our group of weaklings, is so damn positive I'd think she was on drugs, if I thought she could get them here. So just because of her cheery attitude, I place her among the strong. Then there is Flame. She has her very own knight in shining armor for a guard. Not that she needs one—she is unbreakable. I am shocked that the rest of us have made it this far.

I pull out my pad and paper and begin to scribe another letter to Keegan. We would be nearing a year of marriage if I hadn't been taken.

My Dearest Keegan,

I can't imagine what you must be going through not knowing what happened to me. Nine months is a long time. I can only hope that you are still waiting for me, that you believe I will come back to you. This place is hell. I hope our love is strong enough to survive the things that I have suffered here, because the only way I will overcome this is knowing that I have you.

You know, in the beginning, I used to pretend I was with you every time I was with one of them. It worked for a while, but I think my brain caught on and won't let me lie to myself anymore. Each day I am breaking into pieces.

Three more months. I need to survive three more months. I will see you soon. I believe that. I love you so much and can't wait to become your wife.

Yours forever,
Maeve

I don't know if I will ever show these letters to Keegan. Mostly, I write them for myself. They allow me to speak aloud what is on my mind. Keegan really is the very best part of me. We met when his family moved to Dublin. I was eighteen, Keegan was twenty. We hit it off well because we both shared an American and Irish connection. Keegan was born in Dublin, a Flanagan, but grew up in the States. His father is Irish, his mother a famous American actress who met his father while filming a movie in Ireland. I was born to Irish parents, an O'Malley, and I have the red hair and freckles to prove it. I am a ginger through and through. But I am not Irish born. I have citizenship in both countries, but I was born in America, and my family moved back to Ireland when I was in fifth grade. Keegan and I became fast friends, sharing some of our favorite American and Irish customs.

Before I turned nineteen we were a couple. It was only natural that I wanted to marry him. He was what my mother and I called "dashing." Worldly, ambitious, romantic, and adventurous. He was the kind of guy who made you feel alive whenever you were in his presence. I can't remember a moment where he was unkind. In a word, he was perfect. Now, in a few months I will be returning to him—hopefully —and I pray that I am still enough.

Chapter Two
Maeve: Home

I miss the streets of Dalkey, a quaint suburb of Dublin and our little slice of coastal heaven. I realize now how deprived I have been of my sight. For a year we were only allowed to gaze among the walls of The Chamber, unless you count the pool party we had while there, when Mason opened up the skylight and allowed us to feel an actual breeze and catch a view of the cloudy sky above. I don't count that. That was only enough to make us crave what we wanted that much more.

Now I am cruising through the streets of my favorite city, in the back of a sedan, on my way home. I never thought this day would arrive.

Freedom.

Rich and free.

Not that money was ever an issue for me. My family is part of a royal line. On my twenty-fifth birthday I will inherit a fortune, so Mason's four-million-dollar payoff may not mean as much to me as the other girls. But I took it anyway. He owes us millions and more for our year of sex slavery. I wish there was a way to use the money to help me forget. Or we could pool our money together to find him and put him in a cell where he belongs. I know that I am not strong enough for that mission, so I must focus on deleting this trauma from my mind, like I did the first time. Then again, I was just a girl the first time, and my brain had a lot more time to stow away the things that happened to me. But the answer to my path to healing is only a short distance away. Keegan. He can fix me. His love will give me the strength to power through this.

The breeze upon my face is everything to me right now. I don't think I will take another simple pleasure for granted again. When we pull up to my house my stomach is in knots as the nerves creep up on me. Dreaming of returning home and actually being here are two different things. I have wanted to walk up to this house and through my front door more than life, but now that I am here all I want to do is vomit on the floor of this nice sedan. The questions, the uncertainty of returning to my life are all weighing down on me.

I sit in the backseat and stare out at my home. It is nothing compared to the lavish Chamber, but it is beautiful to me. Lush grass that seems to go on forever, with a miniature castle-like structure smack dab in the middle. That is home for me—seven bedrooms, a small theater, ten bathrooms. I'm not rich at all, but Ma and Da are. Their status is one of the reasons we moved back to Ireland, because of what happened to me when we were in the United States. My Da felt he could protect me better in his homeland, but I guess he was wrong.

"Home," I whisper. It is as beautiful as I remember, a painting come to life. Filled with people who love me and have no doubt missed me. My Ma and Da, and twin little brothers, Ailbhe and Lugh.

The driver starts down the long, tree-lined driveway. I shake my nerves and worries. This is my home.

"You can let me out here. I want to walk," I tell him. He starts to get out of the car, but before he can, I throw the door open and take off into the lush grass toward home. Giggles bounce off me as I run full speed toward my family, the home I love so much, and to Keegan. It's April in Dublin. The flowers are in bloom; the trees are bulging with life. I never thought I could miss something as simple as a tree, but I did. If anyone catches me, I will look insane for sure, but I can't resist as I wrap my arms around a healthy, full-grown oak. Of course my arms can't begin to contain its girth. "Hi, Mr. Oak Tree, I'm home!"

I release the oak and proceed to greet and smell the divine purple, pink and red blossoms and bushes. Coming home feels like being reborn. Every scent stronger, every sight brighter.

When I get to the front entry I feel the butterflies. Still, I proceed because there is only love inside. I ring the bell over and over. No one is home. The wind whooshes out of my sails a bit, because I sorta expected a huge and emotional homecoming. Instead I have to walk around the side of the house to find the spare key. It is hidden underneath a plant inside a ceramic elephant, but it's not the cliché hiding place —for ours you have to enter a six-digit code on the side of the elephant, and push down on the garden elephant's trunk in order to access it. Thankfully, the key is there.

I unlock the door and run the spare key back to its hiding spot out of habit. Ma would say, "If you never put the key back, it won't be there when you need it." I miss my ma so much. The smells that are assaulting me are so familiar. This time of year the outside of our home is a floral bouquet for the senses.

Opening the front door is like opening a present on Christmas morning or your birthday, I take a few deep breaths and push the door open. The warm scents of home hit me: my mother's bog-standard candles of warm spices and baked apples. *Mmm.*

If you asked me a year ago if I thought I would ever be here again, see my family again, I would have said that I highly doubted it.

How do you trust a monster?

I guess I—we—should be thankful that we were in the hands of *this* monster. He might have been evil and cruel for taking us away from all that we were, but he never lied to us. We were treated very well, and our release date came like he said it would. Doesn't mean that I don't hate him with every inch of my being, but for my release I thank him.

My home is a mixture of things Irish, from our farmhouse table, Ma's candles, the beautiful tapestries, and my favorite brick stove, to my favorite American things, like our sectional sofa and our monster-sized flat screen television.

It is so strange to feel as if I never left home. Everything is the same. Our kitchen, like most, is the hub for the family. When I enter my family kitchen, I feel the spirit of everyone I love so very much. "Tea. I need tea." If there was one thing that I missed this year it was a good cup of Irish tea. I find the cast iron teapot in its usual spot, fill it with water and wait. "A watched pot never boils," is what my ma always says, but for some reason my attention is on the pot, and the pot alone. Tears well up in my eyes and suddenly this teapot is the single most important thing in the world to me, because it means I am home.

"As I live and breathe." My ma's heavy brogue fills the room.

I dare look up. I know I will fall apart when I see her.

There she is. People say that I am her mini-me, and I never agreed with them until now. Her skin is milky, with a healthy share of freckles like mine. She is lithe, with bright blue-green eyes that are misting as she gazes into mine. In the seconds that follow, each one of my brothers and my da crash into the back of Ma, since she stopped at once.

"Criminy, Melanie, why did you stop like that? I spilled my coffee all over me," my da complains from the end of the line.

"Da, it's Maeve!" Ailbhe shouts, and pushes past Ma, running toward me. Lugh follows close behind. My brothers are the most adorable seven-year-old twins. Identical, with dark hair and blue eyes like our da's. They crash into me.

I squeeze the life out of my baby brothers. How can anyone be so cruel and separate a family like this? I send out a silent prayer to my Chamber sisters for their happy return home. The strong ones who I know will come out on top and the weak ones, like me, who may not survive at all. Then I squeeze the boys even tighter.

It is a dream. For the second time in my life I am reunited with my family. The first time, my brothers weren't born yet. My ma still hasn't moved from the spot where she stopped. Her hand covers her mouth and her eyes continue to rain tears.

The next pair of eyes I see belong to Da. He gazes at me, and lets out a deep breath, one he has most likely been holding onto for the entire time that I have been gone.

"My dear, sweet Maeve." He runs to me and wraps his arms around me and the boys who will probably never let me go.

I look to where my ma was standing and she is gone. "Where did Ma go?"

My da glances back to where Ma was standing. "Follow me. I will show you," he says. His voice is musical and sounds like home.

We walk out of the kitchen and into the sitting room. It is difficult to take steps because the boys won't let me go, and Da has ahold of one of my hands. My ma is kneeling in front of a candle, praying. We stand and watch, before my da guides us to join her. As a family we give thanks for my safe return. When my ma is finished she crawls over to me on her knees and wraps me into an embrace and weeps.

"My dear, sweet daughter, how I prayed for you to come back to us, and you are here. I might have just died and gone to heaven." She wipes her eyes and then my eyes. "Peter, is our darling daughter really here?"

"Yes, love."

Then we all wrap our arms around each other.

My ma, being a strong woman, gathers herself together. "I saw you were brewing up a pot of good Irish tea. I know it's your favorite, my love. Let me dish that up for you."

I follow my da toward the sofas. The boys take a seat on each side of me, so close it would be hard to tell where I begin and they end. My ma comes back with a tray full of tea for the grown-ups and milk for the boys, who still seem to not have acquired a taste for our strong Irish tea.

"What happened to you, Maeve?" My da asks the dreaded question.

I hope I will be allowed to forget this soon, but I am sure everyone in my life will want a recount of the events that happened to me. At least the parts I can repeat.

I clear my throat. "I was exercising at the fitness center like always on my days off modeling jobs. I didn't notice anything out of the ordinary when I walked out to my car. I looked around like you taught me, Da. I even had my pepper spray out. The problem is my capturers were already in my car. I managed to spray one of them in the eyes, but I didn't know there was more than one. Major drawback to having really dark windows." A tear catches in my throat. "I think that the boys should run along for the rest of this story."

Ma's face grimaces when she realizes what that might mean. "Boys, run along. We will send for you in a bit," Ma says.

"But…" They try to stay with me. But my da gives them the look he is famous for and they scoot off.

"The person in the backseat put a cloth to my face and the next thing I know I am on an airplane. This entire time I have been locked away with six other girls. Today is the first day I have been outside."

My da jumps up and sits on my right side. My ma does the same, sitting on my left side.

"I was used for sex." The words choke me on the way out. I break down.

My folks are no strangers to consoling me. They both hold me while we all cry together. "I'm calling the Garda," Da says.

I nod. I knew that was next. I was missing for a year.

Officer Fitzgerald and McKinley arrive within fifteen minutes of our call. I recount my story. Fitzgerald is short and stout and McKinley is tall and rail thin. They look like a caricature drawing come to life. They take notes from my story, and close their pads. Grim looks cross both of their faces.

Fitzgerald speaks up. "You haven't given us much to go on. You've no idea where you were, you were unconscious for most of the flight, and hooded when you were off the airplane, and inside some fortress until today." He shakes his head. "We will do our best, starting with the airport. You had to be on a private plane, so there should be a record," he continues.

Please do your worst. The last thing I need is a visit from the monster.

We thank them and they leave.

"I need to go to bed. I am exhausted," I say.

My parents follow me to my room, and tuck me in. They each plant a kiss on my cheek. "We love you. You rest now, dear."

I am out almost the second they leave my room.

Chapter Three
Maeve: Reliving Nightmares

Five of the seven bookcases slide open, revealing darkened staircases. The five of us who aren't virgins are instructed to take the stairs. I am trembling so hard I might break my bones. Each step I take is a death march. The man downstairs who calls himself Mason makes this place seem like an amusement park, but I promise none of us are amused. There is a draft in the stone stairwell causing me to shiver more. My teeth begin to bang into each other without my control. When I hit the top of the stairs I see that there is a room. Everything is emerald green, accented with gold. A huge bed sits in the middle of the room. I don't need anyone to spell out what that means for me. I realize that I am not alone when I hear someone clear their throat. I spin around and find a young woman standing near what looks like the entrance of a bathroom.

"I am sorry to startle you, miss. I am Iris, and I will be your groomer during your stay here."

Iris is pretty. Tall and thin, with dark brown hair and dark eyes. She has a kind face. "What is that? A groomer?" I ask.

She walks deeper into the green room. "I am here to make your stay bearable. I will keep you groomed and Chamber ready. After you meet your guard, I will take you on a personal tour."

As if on cue, a man walks into the room. He is very attractive as well. I am noticing a theme here. "I am Ridley." He extends his hand and I take it. Even in shock I do what is customarily polite. "I am here to keep you safe. Unless, of course, you fall asleep in your Chamber. Then I am here to fuck your brains out." I snatch my hand out of his. He offers me a menacing smile. "My post is downstairs at the base of your Chamber. There are cameras throughout your room and it is miked. If anything goes down, I will be up here in a flash."

I throw up in my mouth a little.

Can you hold your breath long enough to die? I plan to give that a try. Ridley excuses himself and disappears into the staircase.

"Okay, for the tour. This, of course, is your Chamber. Over here..." Iris walks me to a golden armoire. "Is your pleasure cabinet..."

She opens it, and I cringe. It is filled with dildos, whips, beads — things I have never seen in person. She scoops up a huge dildo and walks across the room. I don't follow her with my body. Only my eyes travel with her. I'm not sure I will be able to remain standing if I move.

"This..." She is standing next to a horse that looks as if it belongs on a carousel. She screws the dildo onto the horse's back. "Is your pleasure pony. You will most likely spend a great deal of time pleasuring yourself for the gentlemen during your stay here."

I hit the ground.

When I wake up there are five men in my emerald room. One of the men picks me up and sets me onto the pleasure pony. "Work, girl," he says.

I can't see his face. I can't see any of their faces, only their erect cocks, all waiting for their turn with me. I sink down onto the pleasure pony. Over and over I plunge the large dildo deep into myself. Tears storm from my eyes. Another faceless cock pulls me from the pony and tosses me onto the bed and all of the cocks converge on me. What started out as five keeps multiplying until the room is full of them, in my mouth, in my ass, my pussy, full of cocks.

I shoot up in bed, my own screams waking me. My door flies open and my ma and da are at my side at once. I can't catch my breath. The sobs are coming out of me in force. My parents don't say a word. What is there to say? They wrap me in love and protection. I can hear the tears they each fight catching in their throats. Their daughter may just be the most unlucky young woman alive. My ma and da get comfortable on each side of me and that is how we fall asleep. With the protection of them, I am able to sleep without any nightmares.

Continue reading Poisoned Ivy

AFTERWORD

Did you love Shattered Sapphire? Be sure to review it on Amazon and let other romance readers know what you thought!

💋 Dionne

MAILING LIST

Did you enjoy *Shattered Sapphire* be sure to join my mailing list and get the inside scoop on new releases, and have access to unreleased short stories about the characters you love!

D.W. MARSHALL'S DARK HEARTS

Want to talk with other romance lovers? Join my Facebook Group, D.W. Marshall's Dark Hearts.

ALSO BY D.W. MARSHALL

The Seven Chambers Series

Stolen Flame

Weeping Violet

Shattered Sapphire

Poisoned Ivy

Eclipsed Sunshine

Cruel Obsessions Series

Twisted Soul

Coming Soon Twisted Heart

The Men of the Seven Chambers Series

Dominic

The Escorts Series

ACKNOWLEDGMENTS

My family for listening to my crazy ideas and staying excited with me. My son Jacksen, for helping me keep my goals ever present and in front of me. My son Spencer, for showing me early on what grinding really means. My husband for cheering me up and telling me that he's proud of me, especially when I'm whining. To my readers, thank you for your kind words and for loving my stories. To my publishing team: The Danielles, Danielle Acee and Danylle Salinas, thank you for cracking the whip when I need it. I swear I thought I was good at multitasking until I became an author, boy was I wrong. But my publishing team helps me juggle and they are amazing at it.

ABOUT THE AUTHOR

D.W. Marshall is a graduate of Tuskegee University. She is a native of California, but grew up in Las Vegas. If you opened her purse you'd find too many pens for one person, lip balm, and the dreaded receipts that never seem to go away.

D.W. loves to read dark *and* sweet romance, fantasy, YA, thrillers, and lives in Las Vegas with her husband, two sons, niece, and her one-eyed Bichon, named Sadie.

https://linktr.ee/dwmarshall